Azanian Bridges

Nick Wood

For Abner, and to the non-repetition of history.

"The most potent weapon in the hands of the oppressor is the mind of the oppressed." – Steve Biko, 1971. (*'I Write What I Like.'*)

Azanian Bridges

Nick Wood

NewCon Press
England

First published in the UK by NewCon Press, April 2016
41 Wheatsheaf Road, Alconbury Weston, Cambs, PE28 4LF

NCP 093 (limited edition hardback)
NCP 094 (softback)

10 9 8 7 6 5 4 3 2 1

ISBN:

978-1-910935-11-8 (hardback)
978-1-910935-12-5 (softback)

Cover Art by Vincent Sammy
Cover layout by Andy Bigwood

Edited by Ian Whates
Interior layout by Storm Constantine

Chapter 1
Sibusiso's Start

I never knew it would be so hard to say goodbye, especially to my father. (I leave him until last.)

"Sala kahle, tata!" I say, bowing my face so he cannot see my eyes.

For a brief moment, he holds me close to him and I can smell the Earth: sweet, sharp sweat and the decades of cattle manure on his skin. His jacket buttons poke into my stomach – he has dressed for this occasion too. He is so like a fragile bird – a *kiewietjie* comes to mind for some reason – but then he pushes me away, turns and walks off in a hurry and without looking back. He has left me with a little gift, a small beige plastic digi-disc, on which I can record the happenings in my life.

I put it in my pocket.

Since when did my father get so old, so delicate, so suddenly?

I look over my brother and sisters' heads to watch his stiff blue-jacketed back disappear into the house. The brown door shuts against yellow brick and the late afternoon sun glints off the corrugated silver eaves and roof.

Behind our master's house, I hear the cows sounding out as a dog barks, unsettling them.

Lindiwe is crying openly but I keep my own eyes dry. I am the eldest son; I am strong.

There is time for one last hug before the taxi arrives.

Mandla grips my arm tightly. "Careful brother," his eyes are almost on a level with my own, despite the three years I have on him, "There is much danger and distraction in the city."

I nod and brush my lips with the back of my left hand to hide my smile: "I hear what you say, Mandla – you repeat Father too – but I will be careful."

He grins and puffs his fifteen-year old chest, which looks increasingly like a solid drum of *utshwala besizulu* - but only the finest of beer.

A high-pitched car hooter sounds behind me. Father had to pay much to have the man detour off his route to come here.

My five sisters wave as I step with difficulty into the crowded taxi; the door is slid fully open, the minibus is silver and muddy brown from the farm track's splatter of early-summer showers.

The driver accelerates before I can sit. I fall into a large woman's lap and realise there is little available seating. She shovels me aside with a large forearm and I sway, trapped between her fat hip and a thin man's sharp thighbone. He wriggles a bit like a contortionist and my buttocks manage to find some sticky leather to ease the weight off my feet.

My grey Sunday slacks stick to the seat, as we sway around and bump over farm potholes.

The *'gamchee'*, as the Cape Coloured people call them, waves a hand towards me from the front seat: "Where you going again, boy?"

"*Fundimiso* College, Im– Imbali," I say, finding it hard to breathe, crushed as I am as the large woman squeezes against me.

The *gamchee* turns to the driver, who is accelerating into a violent right-turn onto the tarred road: "Seems like we have a clever boy in our taxi, hey Smokes?"

Smokes just grunts from under his Man U cap and shakes his dreads. I see he has an OPod plugged into his ears.

I plug an earpiece into my own ears, folding my arms tightly over my old music pod and the rands strapped in a leather purse across my stomach inside my white buttoned shirt, the purse hot and wet against my skin from the late afternoon heat.

The sky still looks clear – no gathering thunderstorm tonight it seems. I glance across at the passengers swaying and talking in front of me. They're arguing about the price of bread.

I am too tired to listen and try to sleep. Keeping my arms

crossed across my hidden money pouch, I doze in fits and starts to random braking, accelerations and Church-Rap from the Crischen-Niggaz.

I finally fall asleep to Muth'fuckas Who Don't Know Jesus...

The fat woman is climbing over me and I see she has a baby hanging off her right hip, swinging it onto her back as she steps outside. It's built like me; it keeps right on sleeping...

Then I see the driver getting out too – what's his name?

I look across to the open door and see I'm the last one inside. I stretch and rub my eyes. My OPod has gone silent.

A big white man with a fierce brown handlebar moustache and blue police cap sticks his head inside: "Out, *kaffir*!"

Hayi no, it must be a roadblock.

I step outside, sweating hard, although the sun is low and the air is cooling.

There's a mellow yellow police van parked in front of us. We're pulled off to the side of the road, traffic whooshing past us and down the hill, down into the smoky valley of umGungundlovu – or Pietermaritzburg as the *boere* like to call the place.

So close, why did they have to stop us now?

Fierce-moustache policeman is going through the driver's papers. Two other black cops are rummaging through our taxi, looking for guns or drugs, probably both.

"Hey, line up!" the white cop shouts, throwing the driver's papers back at him. Smokes, that's his name, catches the papers deftly with a weary shrug of his shoulders and turns back to his cab.

We stand in a ragged line, all nine of us, as he slowly works his way through our *dompas*. My hands are clammy as I pull mine out of my hip pocket.

He moves alongside me and snatches it from my hand; as if angry they've all been in order so far.

I sweat, even though it's getting cold, the sun sinking below the city's smog.

He looks at me and I'm reminded of Ballie Boetze, the big white South African world-boxing champion from several decades ago – whose face has received a nostalgic comeback on TV since his death, advertising Rocket Jungle Weetie-Oats.

"Hey, why you sweating so much, boy, what you hiding?"

"Nothing, sir!" I hate my sweat and my use of 'sir', but all I want is to get to college safely.

"Ach man, they can go!" He slaps my dompas into my open palms.

I see the two black cops are standing behind him, hands on hips, empty.

"Next time I'll give you a bledy fine for over-crowding, hey!" he shouts at us as we climb back into the taxi.

Smokes lights a cigarette, but no one says anything.

This time I find a space next to the window and keep my face averted from the others, watching the lights popping up like fireflies, as the quick dusk deepens into murky darkness.

The rest of the journey is made in a tense silence. As for me, I shake until the end.

I miss my father already.

Chapter 2
Martin's Made

Dan dumps the cardboard box in front of me. Roughly the size of a shoe box, it's packaged tightly in brown paper and yellow duct tape, the words 'Extremely Fragile' scored in red ink over the American stamps of Obama and Malcolm X.

"How the hell did you get that through customs?" I ask.

Dan taps his pale curved nose and smiles: "Let's just say we had to exceed our grant budget a bit."

I grin back at him, aware my heart is starting to race.

Ten whole years of sweat, tears and thoughts are contained in this small, heavy package. What the hell will we do if it doesn't work?

Dan isn't wasting time, he's already cutting through the tape with a wicked pair of scissors. I double-check to make sure his office door is firmly shut.

He tears the paper away, revealing an innocuous-looking plain metallic box. His usually obsessively neat office is littered with scraps of paper, but he doesn't seem to care.

Nor do I.

Unable to sit still, I stand up. I have to do something.

He takes a deep breath and opens the box, unclipping the secured hook that has been inserted on top. Without pausing, he pulls it open.

"It's uh – smaller and duller than I expected," I say.

He grins at the disappointment that must be written over my face.

"Ja, I know – the miracles of miniaturisation. It's amazing how quickly stuff gets smaller and smaller. As for the colour…" He shrugs, "I thought black would be unobtrusive."

"In this country, that's a bloody joke," I crane my neck forward. "They've kept markings to a minimum."

'That's just the top," he says, tilting the box-like cube carefully and cradling its corner as he slides the machine out. "Let's have a proper look at 'Helen', shall we?"

I smile; Helen was Dan's wife, a lawyer with mind-reading abilities that would put any psychologist to shame. "It looks like something that's been dropped out of a fucking plane crash."

Dan wags a finger at me and then, using his right hand to support it, places the box squarely on the table, right side up.

I kneel down on the floor - kneecaps pressing uncomfortably on his checked Formica floor - in order to get a better look at our box. Dan steps to my side of the desk, so that we can both see it clearly.

There are two sets of holes on either side of the box for brain-electrode leads – a power-cord no doubt attaches to the back. The face of the box has an on-off switch on the front, a small power bulb to register current and a big dial with a small digital display on either side – 'Import' on one side, 'Export' on the other.

Apart from that, there is a small power bar display on the right side of the front of the black box, entitled: 'Signal Fidelity.' And, right next to it, a small switch labelled 'record.'

"Record?" I look up at Dan.

He gives a cynical smile. "Jonny, our neuro-engineer, reckoned we could also record captured brainwaves into the neural software."

No wonder he looks sceptical; but Jonny Duke has no equal in this country.

A knock on the door makes both of us jump. It swings open immediately.

A man leans in, a familiar grey-haired and prissy looking man – a polka dot bow tie of all things flowering hideously at the top of his blue shirt and a brown corduroy jacket with leather elbow pads. I am not surprised to see him, perhaps alerted by the faint stench of mothballs before the door opened.

"What on Earth are you doing, Dr. van Deventer, have you

become a Muslim?"

I stand slowly on creaking knees and Dan crosses his arms and grins: "I think you'll find Muslims don't prostrate themselves before anything other than the real Black Stone in Mecca, Dr. James!"

"Ah, Dr. Botha," the old man turns slowly, but not enough to face him directly, looking at him askance. "So how is academia treating you – and what rats are you experimenting on now, here in your Ivory Tower?"

Dan's cheeks stiffen as he clenches his teeth. He takes a slow breath and then smiles sweetly, "What brings you here, my dear Dr. James?"

The senior psychiatrist turns to me: "This afternoon's ward round in the admissions ward has been brought forward to one p.m., so I'm afraid you will have to cut your University visit short."

I feel in my pocket and haul out my cell-phone: "Your PA could have told me that."

He gives a little sniffy chuckle, "Indeed." He looks me up and down, "But given I am your senior I thought it prudent to know what your University business actually is."

He glances pointedly at the Black Box.

Dr. Ronald James has always been proud of his 1820 English settler roots and never fails to 'elocute' carefully, so I weigh up my responding words. Dan is glaring across at me and I know I need to be extra cautious. "I can't say much at this stage, it's still in the experimental phase," I say.

"Oh, is that so?" he draws himself up stiffly and I see he's wearing his usual fluorescent green takkies below carefully pressed brown cotton trousers. "May I remind you, Dr. Van Deventer, that you are a Hospital employee and that we are paying for your time here – I demand more clarity as to what that contraption actually is."

Funny, those shoes, as if part of him rebels against the conformity which covers the rest of him in such staid, traditional, stultified clothing.

As if he would like to run another race, walk another walk? Still, he can be a real dog with a bone, so I decide to level with him, giving him both barrels in the hope he would scoff it away: "A thought box, a neuro-physiological device that both reads and transmits brainwaves via mirrored magnetic pulses, focused over Broca's area particularly..."

Whatever else he may be, he's not a stupid man. His face crumples in slow amazement, mixed with growing incredulity. He hesitates and I enjoy his speechlessness, just for the moment it lasts. His features finally settle with a widening realisation in his eyes, but his words are still laced with scepticism. "Ah yes, I remember your joint papers from a few years ago when you were working here – speculative but ambitious stuff indeed, the route to mind-reading."

I gesture to the Box proudly, somehow strangely wanting him to believe in me.

He raises an eyebrow: "It works?"

Dan steps across, picks the box up and places it carefully back in its container:

"We don't know, there's still testing to be done."

Dr. James laughs, a short fruity chuckle: "Well, have fun trying to get that one through ethics, boys!" He turns to leave, but glances over his shoulder: "One p.m., Dr. van Deventer."

He leaves quietly, but I can still smell mothballs and stale tobacco.

Dan looks at me, fiddling the securing lever on the container. "He may be an arsehole, but he's right you know. It's going to be a job getting this through ethics – given the focus on Broca's and the importance of language on thought, a dry run with animals may not tell us much."

I stare back: "How about we two do it?"

He gives a wry smile: "I see there's also a paper or two coming out about a possible weak link between deep brain stimulation and tumours."

"Oh," I say.

He picks the box up and offers it to me.

"What?" I say, cradling it dumbly.

"You work in a place where people are readily available, Marty; I think you can do this – even if it's off the record, as it were."

"You serious?"

His cheeks are even tighter and I know that look well – he used to wear it when he took his ball home at school, if the game didn't go his way.

This time though, he is offering me the ball, although he seems to let go with reluctance.

"What's stopping us?" he shrugs, "The Yanks got away with Tuskegee. This is a whole lot better than that; I'm pretty sure the link with brain tumours is spurious."

We weigh each other up quietly and I know he's not going to take the risk to find out just how spurious.

"All right then," I say, wondering if I'm going to regret this.

"Oh, and Marty?" He cups his chin with his right hand, index finger sliding up alongside his nose. I know that body language from school. "Take bledy good care of – uhhh, our machine, okay?"

I nod and leave with a slight shiver, even though our school years are long behind us.

Chapter 3
Sibusiso's Learning

I like my history teacher.

She's a short skinny woman, an Indian, a bright green headscarf hiding her hair, so I assume she's a Muslim. My mother may not have approved of her then - but that matters little now, for she herself is long gone.

Dr. Wadwalla moves and fidgets quickly in front of us, pointing to the screen above her head at the first lines displayed from our recommended history text.

"Well, teachers to be – what's wrong with this opening sentence?"

There are about thirty of us crammed into this small room, the floor sloping down towards the wooden lectern. 'State of the art' we've heard – as good as any white teachers in training get – separate yes, but equal.

Hah.

I like our history teacher because she asks questions, instead of telling us what to think – and she doesn't hide behind the lectern, like others do. I frown at the words highlighted in red on the overhead screen, but don't know the answer.

Bongani next to me raises his hand – several others have done so too, but Ms. Wadwalla points to him first.

I wonder if she notices me.

Bongani stands up, pausing a bit for dramatic effect. His chest is puffed slightly, as if he is indeed confident he knows the answer.

"South African history did not start in 1652,' he says.

"Yesss, exactly!" she taps the desk in front of her with the long white plastic pointer, then lays it on the desk and crosses her arms. "So which of you can tell me when South African history started?"

There is silence.

She moves to the front of her desk, almost standing amongst the front row. "No one?"

There is a small drone near the back on the right – I turn to see a man at the back showing the girl next to him something on his phone.

Dr. Wadwalla ignores them, although they are sitting right under a 'Cells Off' sign.

"Well, I suppose it's early days for you all yet. The answer is no one knows exactly, but archaeological evidence suggests Africans have been here for a lot longer than that – and Van Riebeeck was greeted and provisioned by some Khoi-San 'strandlopers', many of whom were later shot by the white settlers for their charity."

She picks up a small screen-sorter gadget from the desk and clicks – a drawn picture of a curly-haired coloured man appears on the screen.

"The fruits of the arrival of Van Riebeeck, seasoned by a later dose of slave spice from the east and we have the so-called 'coloured' people, drawn in the book here as if they are a separate and set race." She pauses: "Any so-called 'coloureds' here?"

We crane our neck around the room, but no one puts their hands up.

She smiles, looking a little sad while she does so: "Well, most of us may have some 'coloured' blood in us – anyone remember the history of World War Two?"

A forest of arms goes up, including my own.

This time she laughs: "Remember the villain of that war – he believed in racial purity didn't he? And look where he ended up."

She clicks the screen off.

"Your group-work for now? Get together in your tutorial groups and discuss how many things are wrong in the first chapter of your book. Choose a group-leader to feedback to us all in twenty minutes time."

"Miss!" A striking young woman with a cropped head in the

front row is almost standing up in her eagerness to ask something, but Dr. Wadwalla seems to anticipate her question. (I do not know if correctly so.)

"Why are we using this book? Because no other book has been allowed by the government. I'm hoping you lot will end up writing a newer and better one, one day, one day..." She claps her hands: "Right now, get into your groups".

I look across at the crop-haired woman, wishing she were nearby, so that she could join our group.

The lights of the club strobe like rainbows across our faces, the digital beat of kwela-rap drowning our voices.

So Bongani and I start to shout about our history class but I can tell Mandla is bored with that. (He's short and skinny and is nothing like my brother, although his name still hurts a bit, a constant reminder of old memories of play-wrestling and brotherly jokes.)

Mandla rolls his eyes at us: "Enough work, dull Jacks – how about some *ntombis* – there are a couple of pretty girls over there looking our way."

I follow where he points, but see the table across the way is frequented by two smart looking women – sporting sophisticated tattoos that shift across their face in day-glo orange and green, advertising Bafana Bafana and GoBeef. They must have paid a fortune for those moving tattoos, although maybe they're pirated imitations. The women are engrossed in talk with two big men and neither of them glances our way, but I notice how well the women fill their jackets; particularly the nearest one, who looks vaguely familiar, although she has her back to us.

"So, what say you all?"

Bongani throws a beer mat at him: "Don't be stupid – we didn't come here for a fight."

Mandla swats it aside, gets up and suddenly swoops on Bongani from behind, putting him in a headlock. Bongani retaliates with a punch aimed behind his head, but Mandla dodges it. Old sparring partners it seems, although Bongani is gurgling with his windpipe cut off and his eyes are bulging. He picks up a knife from the table in front of him: "Stop – it – Mandla!"

Mandla lets go with a laugh. "Hey, man, always serious, why don't you just relax and have a bit of fun? It's three against two with the table next door."

Bongani coughs over the table, massaging his throat.

"Not really," I say. "Have you seen the women's jackets?"

Mandla turns and is silent for a moment: "Oh," he says, swivelling back to us,

'Well they're ugly bitches anyway."

The slogans are stitched in lurid green on the women's black fake leather jackets – *ukubuyisa isithunzi sobusuku*, Safety at Night – an amaZulu Amazonian women's group, feisty with their fists and feet. Even in the country, we've heard of them. In addition, the two big men look to have seriously soured our odds in a fight. Besides, Father always told me that knives and fists belonged to a bankrupt mind. He himself was always polite and careful with his words and the little money he had.

Mandla reaches down to grab Bongani's throat again, but he is too slow. Bongani thrusts an elbow behind him and Mandla doubles over; Bongani's aim is true.

The nearest woman comes over to us; her cropped head accentuates her plain but rippling face. Where have I seen her before?

"He's been an idiot, has he?" she dismisses the groaning Mandla, clutching his crotch. "If you boys fancy being men, how about coming to this? I'm Nombuso, by the way."

She slaps a leaflet down on the table and I recall where it is that I've seen her before – she's the girl who was straining to ask a question at the end of class. *Hayi*, how night, clothes, and activated fluorescent mobile tattoos can change someone.

She turns her back and struts back to her table, not waiting for a response.

The leaflet is a call to attend a protest march. At the bottom of the list of sympathetic academics due to attend a name jumps out at me: Dr. Fariedah Wadwalla.

Our history teacher.

I catch Bongani's eye. He shrugs: "Why the hell not?"

Mandla has settled into a chair alongside us. He's still wheezing and bent over the table, almost dropping his face into a glass of beer. "The *boere* will be there you know," he says, "Bringing dogs and guns and pain."

Bongani shrugs, puffing himself up slightly: "We will show them who is boss.

This is our land – we should not be bowing to them."

Mandla looks up and he has sweat on his face, which seems somehow paler in the club's lights: "You don't mess with the *boere*."

I am troubled. It is not like Mandla to be cautious.

Bongani just laughs: "What has suddenly turned you into an old woman?"

Mandla stands up and slugs the last of his beer: "My oldest brother died in detention... And my *gogo* is braver than any man alive." He walks out of the club without looking back, leaving us in strained silence.

Bongani forces a laugh: "Are you ready for another beer?"

But I have no more appetite. I stand to leave too.

"Where are you going?" asks Bongani.

"To bed," I pick up my coat, not looking back as I manoeuvre through the tables.

There is one couple on the circular dance floor, cuddling to the techno-beat.

I skirt past them to the door.

The walk to our dormitory is not far. All I can do is think of my mother.

She died too. No, the *boere* didn't kill her. She got Aids from a rapist. We found the rapist and our local butcher castrated him.

But my mother died slowly all the same.

Bongani is alongside me as I open our dormitory door,

knowing better than to say anything.

Mandla is already in bed.

In the end, all three of us decide to go: Mandla mutters he will make his *gogo* proud. (As for me, Dr. Wadwalla will be there too – and the cop's face on the ride in to college still shouts inside my head! I need a way to silence him.)

Mandla flashes a hand-sign to passing taxis and one screeches to a stop. The taxi is almost full as usual, four young men and two women with furled banners, an older woman with shopping. The van swerves around a few burning tyres as we near the settlement.

One of the young women mumbles to her male neighbour they'd caught an informer last night and neck-laced them – I stop listening and turn to stare out of the window, rocking slightly and tightly between Mandla and Bongani.

We skip past the silent array of new and few government box houses, designed to prove equality and to undermine resistance. We slow as we approach the informal settlement where most people live, shanty houses thrusting up defiantly from the dust.

The crowd is already milling around the point where the muddy road peters out, leading nowhere but to that sprawling shantytown. There are several hundred shacks it seems, tilted and splayed thinly in corrugated sheets and chipboard against the summer storms, spread in a chaotic and smelly space. No running water, waste both of and from humans lies in a heaped pile under bushes to our right; the people have made an attempt to keep the place clean. No council collection comes through - the police and bulldozers are no doubt expected first.

The gathering crowd itself looks close to a thousand, although I am not a good estimator of numbers, coming as I do from a small village near the Underberg. Still, there are more than I expected. I crane my neck to gaze through the crowd, but do not see Dr. Wadwalla.

Banners are being unrolled and I hear the snap of a few illegal cam-phones, providing photos of resistance for downloading and spitting through State firewalls.

There are a few rough table stalls with drink and food – some water, beer, and even a few crates of Croke that may have accidentally slipped off a lorry. The food looks like beef meat and samp – appetizing, but expensive at twenty rands a plate. (It looks like the women and the sharply dressed man in a cream suit are not catering for locals or students – or perhaps they are just optimistically testing the waters, as the day is young.)

I scan the banners – ubiquitous ANC flags of course, but a few PAC and even one or two Inkatha, from their split-off revolutionary wing that defies Buthelezi and a Bantustan state. There is a scuffle as someone hoists a banner unfamiliar to me – Mandla points it out and explains patiently to me, the country *plaasjapie*. Black power, one settler, one bullet and a new state to be called Azania, heralded in by The Azanian Peoples' Organisation.

We jostle for space as time passes, the crowd appears to be loosely milling around a central platform of raised wooden pallets and they've even been able to rig up a microphone on a stand, attached to a mobile generator running off petrol, the smell of fuel cuts across the stink of shit.

Bongani kicks at a stray dog smelling his shoe and I glare at him. We look for a closer space amongst the mess of people, some talking, others arguing loudly.

Bongani pushes a route through to the platform, but we get held up by a large group of Inkatha Revolutionary men, who have linked arms and turn to glower at us.

We hang back – I feel young, a wafting boy.

Bongani glances at his cell: "They're twenty minutes late."

Mandla laughs dryly: "Haven't you heard the term Africa time? These things are always late."

Bongani curses as he lifts his right shoe, wiping at it with a scrap of newspaper he's picked up. The stench of shit hits my nose even harder.

I look forward though; the men ahead of us are stirring. Someone has stepped up onto the wooden platform. We turn to stare over bobbing heads, some people already starting to chant Struggle slogans.

I am grateful for my six foot plus – I have a good view of ... her.

It is the young woman, Nombuso, from last night. She cannot be more than a few months older than me, but she stares across this crowd so coolly, as if she were forty years old.

'*Amandla!*' she shouts, fisting the air.

There's a ragged roar of 'Awethu' in response, but I see a few competing banners jostling for space on the edge of the crowd. As for us, only about midway in as befits late arrivals, I am glad for the space to retreat if necessary.

There is a sharp whine from the mike – feedback – and the young student covers it with her hand. As the mike quietens, Nombuso opens her mouth to speak, but all that is heard are... sirens.

People shout; movement causes us to turn towards the road behind us.

Convoys of mellow yellow police vehicles arrive. Some of them have netted grilles with attached dog boxes. The sirens cut through the shouts and screams, the vans fanning out into a semi-circle, churning to a halt in the mud.

Our route is cut off – the only way out is backwards, through the shacks.

Policemen leap out, automatic rifles in hand, taking cover aggressively behind their vehicles.

A fizz near me; a man lighting a bottle: a Molotov Cocktail? I've heard of these, but never actually seen one. I stare. It is burning too quickly and the man drops it with a curse, stamps it out.

Dogs bark in front of us – Dobermans and Alsatians on leads scrabbling in front of the dog-handlers, like bulls eager to gore us. Behind us, a few pitiful yammerings of township dogs, but none of them come forward to pick up the challenge from the beefy *boere* dogs.

A fat *boer* steps forward holding a loud-hailer, shiny metal pins on his blue uniform. He has a thick handlebar moustache framing his shaking jowls. His voice is strangely high pitched and crackles through the loud hailer. "This is an illegal gathering. You have five minutes to peacefully dis-perrrse!"

"*Amandla!*" the word cracks across the place, with an electronic force. It is Nombuso, mike in hand, standing in defiance, legs starting to pump the slow rhythm of the *toyi-toyi*, "*Oessss, oesss, oesss, oesss…*"

The crowd starts to respond, although a few at the back are running into the shacks, as if knowing what is to come.

I catch the chant '*umshini wami*', a few women are ululating a Thandiswa chorus, but I don't see any guns in the crowd.

I am being pushed forward towards the front, but there is nowhere to go.

The shouts rise, the crowd seemingly solidifying around Nombuso on the platform, who is ululating into the mike, right fist raised, shaking.

I crouch down, wishing my father were with me. Mandla, though, reaches for mud, sifting it in search of a stone or brick. Bongani has gone, threading backwards through the crowd.

I crouch, too scared to move.

A harsh line of white men in blue in front of me – *they* have guns – every single one of them. Their vicious dogs paw the air eagerly.

We are not given anywhere near three minutes.

A 'woosh' and a spray of objects flies amongst us from mobile launchers hidden behind the vans. A bang hurts my ears and clouds of stinging smoke swirl around us – some people have already wrapped scarves around their faces and are moving forwards, sticks and stones in hand. Me, I kneel in the mud choking on the teargas, eyes burning, seeing little.

A rattle of gunshots and they are upon us – dogs with huge dripping teeth and men slashing with whips, truncheons, sjamboks. God, some even have the latest electro-hammers, frizzing as they hit. I scramble to my feet; a nearby explosion knocks me back into the mud and I curl up, arms wrapped around my sticky head. A woman wails as she dashes by, another trips over me and falls with a scream, scrabbling to get away.

Off to one side, out of the corner of my eye, a spray cannon spurts purple dye onto people.

It's over within four minutes, but they seem like years. I check my blurred watch and look around, eyes still seeping.

Smoke is settling into the ground.

The police are loading a group of men and women into their vans, but I – and a few others – am left alone to grovel on the ground. I stay down, not wanting to be noticed, but my head is aching and sore.

It is then that I see him, lying on his back, sprawled only a few paces from me. I notice with horror his mouth is open, unmoving. Mandla! I cradle his head, but see his left eye is missing, just a bloody volcano in his weirdly distorted face. I shake him, but his mouth flops, with no breath. I see bloody grey goo on my trousers. The back of Mandla's head is oozing.

I clutch him and scream. The fuckers used live rounds!

A man touches my shoulder. He still looks neatly dressed, but with traces of mud and blood on his cream jacket sleeve.

"Come, brother, have something to eat," he holds a sagging plate of beef and *samp*, but all I can do is gag.

"Sibusiso, is Mandla...?" I see Bongani's feet, but do not look up.

"Yes," I say.

Mandla is dead.

I do not return to class.

When Mandla is buried, I do not go either, guilty though I feel. Twelve others are buried with him and there is much shouting and singing, but the police let them alone this time.

Or so Bongani tells me; standing beside my bunk, he pokes me with his ruler and tells me to stop being so lazy and get up.

It hurts me, although I mask my face. My father has always taught us to work hard. So I try to pull books into bed with me, but the words just blur in front of me and I shut them before the print runs.

I scrub myself in the shower twenty three times over the week and still I feel Mandla's blood and brains on my legs, although when I look hard, it is just my own raw skin, so I climb back into bed with waves of tiredness I cannot resist.

Bongani brings me food but I am too tired to eat, so I just sleep, dreaming little.

I lose count of days and faces before me, but there is something about this knock at the door I cannot ignore.

The knock is short, sharp and persistent; pulling me from my sleep like a *sangoma* pulls spirits from the shadows. I surface to the sound; the 'tah-tah-tahing' pulling my soul into my body. It is hard, but I drag myself up and stagger towards the door.

I know that knock.

I pull the door open, hearing a familiar shuffling step on the other side. For the first time since Mandla died, my blood burns in my body.

"Sibusiso?" It is Father, face creased with concern, hat in hand, dressed in his thin grey suit for the city. A special suit it is, grey like stone, worn at Church too and like the lasting rock beneath us all.

I can only cry like a baby as he supports my wretched body to a chair, although I have six inches over him – tall, just like my mother, he always said. My height means nothing now, for I am a squalling new-born before him, body shaking as I curl-up in the chair, unable to talk. He sits perched on the side of the chair and just holds my shoulders, as my body eventually runs out of tears.

"Your friends are worried, son, as is the college nurse."

Nurse? I saw no nurse.

"She said you were not responding to her, no matter what she said, so she called the farm and the *baas* came to tell me."

I peer up at him in shame, fingers spread across my eyes.

"I have heard you lost a friend. This is sad. But life goes on – and so must we."

I hear Father's words, but I cannot move. I tell my legs to move, but they stare at me in stubborn silence. I open my mouth, but nothing comes out. I have nothing left inside me, my blood cooling again, slowing in my veins like curdling milk. I bend over, wanting to die.

They do not let me. I feel powerful arms gripping me on both sides, lifting me up as if I was sister Thanda's favourite doll. Big men they are, uniformed in medical blue and they carry me out into the corridor, Father following – and for the second time I have ever known him, his cheeks are wet.

Even in mother's death, he had still been strong for us all.

Mother!

Faces float in front of me, at me, as I am marched down the corridor. I realise I am in shorts and T-shirt, my night pair that I have no idea how long I have been wearing. I try to remember who the people are, but they float before me like ghosts. I cannot hold onto anything, but feel blood in my elbows freeze beneath the grip of these two strong men.

There is an ambulance parked in the college space, door open, but it looks like a police van, so I dig my heels in, but with no reward. They lift me as if I were made of paper and step in, alongside me. There is a mattress, but I will not lie down. The biggest man holds out his hand and pulls Father in behind me. Father does not look at me anymore and I feel yet another small death inside me, like something has broken – but it is distant and numb.

We drive then, but with no siren; softly, softly through the streets, as if off to a picnic. But I sway against the men on both sides of me, on the seated platform along the side of the ambulance, watching my father sway on the other side, looking backwards through the rear window at the cars and people we leave behind us.

I stare too, for my own father does not seem to see me, but I notice little of anything, with no sense of where we are going.

Nor do I care.

The ambulance swings in through a wide gate and chugs up a hill. There are trees and buildings lining the road but we soon grind to a halt.

The back door of the van rattles open and I see a thickset nurse looking at me, smiling in a way that for the barest of moments, reminds me of my mother.

She gestures to us: "Come on then, Sibusiso, welcome to Fort Napier Hospital."

I know now why Father will not look at me. He has brought us to the local mental asylum. He has not come to take me home. Surely he will not leave me here?

Surely, surely, surely?

They have to drag me out and I cannot see where Father has gone.

Chapter 4
Martin's Case

Silence...

Silence shrinks an already small room and I stare at the young man who will not talk, wondering how I reach out across the space between us, how to make his words flow. He stares across to the picture on the wall behind me: his eyes are hooded, his body is slumped. The room is a tight box of peeling institutional yellow, mould-flicking corners of the ceiling, the narrow walls groaning with a history of mad voices . . . or so I've been told. The young man's head is cocked, as if he's listening. Perhaps the voices in the wall have overwhelmed him. Me, I've never heard them, sitting as I am on the right side of this small square desk, panic button comfortably within range on the wall next to me.

"What do you hear, Sibusiso?" I ask, normalising his experiences, just in case.

He flicks a glance to my mouth, as if unsure that's where the voice has come from, but his eyes scan back behind me.

How indeed to build a link between us? I swivel on my higher chair to look at the picture locking his gaze. It's an old photograph I'd taken perhaps a decade or so back, at the turn of the new millennium. It's of a rope bridge with snared base planks, swinging over the Umgeni River. An empty bridge, too treacherous to walk on or cross, with an angled view of the green and distant slope on the other bank. The glass frame keeps the picture from deepening a further yellow and curling at the edges.

Reflected lines of hot sunlight spill in through the slats of drawn blinds, making it hard to see the picture clearly. I know it by heart though – that and the similar but different one in my bedroom at home – the Umgeni Bridge: a place of wild voices, a place of beginnings.

So I stand up, hitch the picture off the hanging nail, and turn to hand it to him.

"Do you like it?" I ask.

He holds the picture, studying it for moments and then he cranes his neck back in order to look up at me. I stand waiting.

"Did you take it, Doctor?"

Ah – a personal question; we're trained to divert those. "What would it mean to you if I did take it?" I ask.

To my surprise, he just chuckles a little to himself. The nurses had said he was responding to the amitriptyline; he'd even managed a supervised weekend out recently.

He leans back to look up at me again.

"I would just like to know whether you've been there and seen this, Doctor."

"Yes," I say; if in doubt, keep it honest and short.

"Would I be allowed to go there and see this for myself too, Doctor?"

"Um, you've only just been home for a weekend, Sibusiso." I sit down, now that a flow of conversation has opened between us. "Why would you want to go?" Why does he ask what we both know is impossible? And it's a bloody high bridge too...

Sibusiso Mchunu sits up a little straighter, the creases in his neat green psychiatric overalls twisting into fresh angles across his lean body. "I never said I want to go, just am I allowed to go, if I were well enough, Doctor?"

"I don't think so, Sibusiso..."

The reason hangs between us like a damp, dark unspoken secret. I get up to switch on the hanging naked bulb overhead so that we can see each other better, the green shades leaking humid heat and light, but keeping the bulk of the sun at bay. I wish the afternoon thunderstorms would gather more quickly.

Perhaps safer verbal territory would help too. "So, tell me something you may have enjoyed doing on your weekend out then, Sibusiso." I sit down and watch his face; he is alert and watchful in return. Keep it close to home; keep it fun, especially with a young man recovering from psychotic depression.

"I – I went to listen to a band playing music at one of our local shebeens. It, uh, was good stuff, Doctor. They played old covers of Aretha Franklin, Stevie Wonder, Gil Scott-Heron and even some old mbaqanga township jazz."

Sibusiso's tongue clicks over the last word, leaving me slightly perplexed, slightly distanced. I recognise the first two names and wonder if the third person referred to was also… black. No, the word was still not to be mentioned – here, at least, race and colour would not be an issue.

So, keep playing it safe, encourage his words – for, in the end, all talking should help. That's the faith of my job. "What did you enjoy most about the music, Sibusiso?"

"That…" Sibusiso sucks in a breath and leans forward slightly: "The fact that black people make such wonderful music and more…"

I smile awkwardly and lean back in my chair. What to do, how to respond? I am a liberal Afrikaner, non-racialist in my attitude. For me, colour is not an issue, not here, not now.

I weigh him up with my eyes – he is sitting forward, eyes wide but respectfully averted, waiting for an answer with a slight twist to his lips.

He raises this mindfully – still, follow the patient, as they say. "So… What does this mean to you?"

Sibusiso flashes me a fleeting look that takes flight like a cagey springbok, dropping his head into his hands, palms up on the table between us. His head is shaven short, the back of his head scarred with a swollen weal as if he'd been beaten in the recent past. By whom, though?

"Sibusiso?" I chime the name delicately, to emphasise both respect and concern.

He stays bowed, silence pooling onto the table.

Is this a signal indicating a therapeutic rupture, presumably around the question of what it means to be both black and to have (musical) achievements… and perhaps my inadequate response?

I sigh. Shall I call in a Zulu nursing staff member to take him back to the ward?

No, that'll be a message that I've given up... and I don't give up on anyone, even if they're just a young Bantu man. I must keep trying to span this experiential chasm that separates us; try and reel him back into this room with words. And, if words do indeed fail, there's always the machine, my machine, my Bridge of Feelings.

I lean across the table until I am close to his scarred head, recoiling a little at the sharp smell of sweat. Was this a sign of deteriorating personal hygiene, a cultural factor, or poverty? Ashamed at my ignorance, I decide I need to confront this silence.

"I'm sorry, Sibusiso, did I say something wrong?" (I am careful not to touch him.)

Silence continues to drip off him in sick emotional waves.

I lean back to breathe more easily. How can I use words to step across the huge gulf that divides us? He had even initially refused to talk to fellow Zulu nursing staff, perhaps afraid they might be government informers. All reports suggest he may be a 'comrade', an anti-apartheid activist, although he had denied that of course in his few, terse words on admission. Here, our task is to make him better, not to vet his political views or activity. I stay neutral; dispassionate, scientific. Psychology is politically impartial in South Africa – even if we have no trained black Zulu psychologists to see Sibusiso either.

There is just me... I stand in frustration. Perhaps he thinks I'm connected with the S.A.P. Special Branch – white man that I am and no matter how much I emphasise confidentiality. My words seem too feeble to convince him otherwise. Just... just perhaps my Feelings Box can heal this rupture, span this gap? It's almost ready; one final test at home tonight and I can smuggle it in tomorrow... if it works.

I look down at the young man's hunched body.

"Sibusiso?"

Sibusiso looks up; his face is stained and shiny with tears. "It – it means the world to me, Doctor."

Ahhh... He's answered my earlier question. Slowed response though, perhaps indicating psychomotor retardation – does his medication need to be increased, after all?

The Umgeni rope bridge photograph lies face down between us, hidden, just a tan cardboard backing in view.

I touch his shoulder lightly and pick the photograph up, putting it back on my office wall.

I'll smuggle the Feelings Box in tomorrow then, if I have to, despite Doctor James. I am old enough to make my own choices.

Outside, thunderstorms are clearing and cooling the air, although the sky is also darkening with the storm and the onset of night.

Safe within the comfort of my small house I hold Jacky, my retriever cross, my cheap *brak* tight, as she struggles in my arms. Wires lace down from our scalps to the Black Box at my feet. I stroke her and murmur in her floppy ears.

This is the warm blue leather couch where we usually sit in peace and watch an evening's TV, skipping past ongoing news flashes summarising the never-ending State of Emergency; the continuing collapse of the rand. New threatening news for us too, we are told - Obama and Osama to meet the Soviet bloc in Peace Talks above the Berlin Wall, as the Soviet Union tires of thirty years of haemorrhaging men into their Afghan ulcer.

I switch the TV off, wondering if the calming couch associations will reassure Jacky, as she scrabbles and scratches at my chest. I take a deep breath and switch the foot-square box-machine on at my feet. Nothing happens; my brain fails to swing into the space separating our different bodies, our separate brains.

I growl with puzzlement, fear, restriction, even a little cold pain, but warmed by sweaty human smells and image flashes of meaty chunks dropping from pink familiar smells. Chunks not here though, body sore, warm smell is squeezing, fear rising, snarls from outside monster…

Arms let go and I scramble under the couch yelping, ripping the electrode-cap free from my/her head. With short, ragged gasps, I clutch at my ribs and lean forward on the couch. The arms are… mine.

I am… Martin Van Deventer, neuropsychologist. Doctor Van Deventer, one of the co-inventors of the 'Feelings Box', the 'Empathy Enhancer' – an EE machine and… it works, it sure as hell works! I must tell Dan…

I stroke the leads that trail from my scalp-cap to the machine, vine-feeders of emotional images from another species. Dogs do see colours, despite having only two visual cones… Or does this come from being filtered through my own brain? Dear God, but this machine could change the whole world, let alone this depressing, ravaged, racialist country.

"Jacky," I call her out from under the couch. She comes reluctantly, trembling, confused. I lift the cap that she'd pulled loose but she gives a brief yelp and retreats under the couch again. Okay then, I'll just have to keep pairing the cap with meaty treats to reinstate a Pavlovian pleasure association for her. Eventually in the future she should yet again lick her small, brown animal-shelter chops, every time I pick up the electrode-cap.

I stroke the chunky Black Box Dan and I cobbled together over the years with carefully filtered research funds. 'Our Empathy Enhancer' up until now had only delivered brief canine flashes of experience; smells that drifted up like vague colours of dried piss from deserted night time telephone poles. I crane down under the couch to tickle Jacky's throat with the fingers of my right hand – she'll eventually forgive me as usual, although now I'll be able to check whether she's forgiven me for sure.

But is it right to assume such forgiveness? Is it right to coerce such participation?

I check the dials on the machine. I had the settings to my cap on 'import' but it is theoretically possible to switch it to an interchange of import and export, an actual swapping of visceral experiences via mutually enhanced and transmitted brain wave responses. (Does this imply there may be neurones that act as experiential mirrors in the mammalian brain? A flaky hypothesis indeed, I know, but some hard evidence is gathering.)

This would still need someone else to independently verify it – and that means another human participant. It might be risky indeed if Dan and I were to try it on each other.

But there is no way I will get permission to use the Empathy Enhancer (EE™) on another person without rafts of peer-reviewed papers to bolster its safe use and our claims. Doctor James remained deeply suspicious of the process, warning me of its dangers during our last session.

"Some boundaries are sacred," he'd said, before admonishing me for not adequately working my divorce through and unconsciously inflicting my 'issues' on patients, especially the white people I saw over weekends in private practice.

But, why does anyone have to know? There'd also be far less fuss if it was a black person… and I know just the man, I think.

But is it right to assume such participation? And can one fairly ask someone, a young Bantu man certified for treatment, within this current psychiatric power structure?

Outside, the storm continues to shout at the house, so I close all the curtains, finding it hard to control my shivering. Jacky trails behind me, whining.

Sibusiso eyes the machine straddling the table between us with obvious doubt.

"It looks like a box the Security Police would use."

I look at him with surprised shock; forthright views indeed for an endogenously depressed patient, especially a black one. But the night nurses did report he'd been more talkative this morning, more assertive.

"It's okay, Sibusiso, I've tried it on myself – it doesn't hurt, it only amplifies your brain waves and enables me to understand your experiences more easily; it works better than any language could."

"What's wrong with my English, black man that I am?" Sibusiso slumps in the chair again, his eyes veiling over.

I knew I would have to engage him quickly, before he regressed further into a depressed stupor. "Stand up, let's move around a bit," I call. Behavioural activation always helps alleviate mood-based psychomotor retardation.

"*Ja baas*, have you been in the army, *korporaal?*" He stands, but sullen, angry and hostile.

This is not going well. I hesitate, unsure of whether his question is seriously meant or a bit of loaded sarcasm. But he continues to stand and stare at me directly, as if in defiance of cultural respect for his elders, waiting…

I smile to break the tension: "We're here to treat you, not me – your family were worried and brought you here because you'd stopped eating."

Sibusiso shook his head: "No, it doesn't work like that. You expect me to share things, hurtful things, dangerous things, yet you say nothing about yourself, nothing about who you really are away from your work? And the white army patrol our streets, shooting and whipping us."

Is this where his head injury comes from?

Silence…

I sense there is no way forward without a big step of trust, a leap of faith.

"No, Sibusiso, I've never been to the army. I'm a secret draft dodger, a good few years back now. I've moved addresses many times and they've given up chasing me – at least, I hope they have, with all their energies in the… black townships, as you say." The word 'black' sticks to my tongue like glue, but Sibusiso has given me enough cues he wants me to verbalise colour, although I still worry it polarises us…

He watches me and relaxes just a little. Then he chuckles, looking around the dingy yellow room: "Well, if you speak the truth, I can probably be sure this room is not bugged."

Is this one reason why his words have been so guarded, so hard to come by? It seems behavioural answers lie not just in a man's mental state, but in their surroundings too. There's a wide gulf between us indeed, even in this cramped and stale room, where we're standing so close we can smell each other.

Sibusiso is sweating, although the sun's mid-morning heat has yet to build strongly. He stretches his arms in response to mine and looks down on me from across the table; he's tall, thin and powerful. I feel the weight of early middle-age years and the spread of my stomach: "Shall we sit again?"

He takes the back of his chair and moves it, appraising me coolly from a standing height as my own chair squeaks, swivels and spins unexpectedly beneath me.

"I'll do this on one condition," he says.

I stabilise and root myself by planting my shoes firmly against the concrete floor, grasping the table in front of me.

"What's that?" I look up to capture his glowering gaze.

"You must go first, Doctor," he says.

Argh, I'd not expected this.

I can see by his stare this is not negotiable. I hesitate, racking my brain for a therapeutic response that would open him up again, a psychological jujitsu phrase that would put me back in control, with therapy moving forward as planned.

"Okay," I say. That's not it! (But what else can I say; who else will agree to do this?)

I take a deep breath and clip the primary cap onto my scalp. He watches me closely; his eyes measuring mine more than they did yesterday.

I hold the second cap up to him and he flinches away. "You can't read me if you're not connected," I say.

He lifts a warning finger: "Promise me you do it the way I want."

I nod and fumble with clipping the electrodes in place, glad he's had his head tightly shaved since coming onto the ward. I am sweating too, even though it is not as hot as yesterday, a drop of sweat falls on the table between us, my collared shirt sticks to my back.

We face each other over the Box, which is plugged in, green dials flashing.

"Ready?" I say, breathing deeply and dreading I am breaking ethical codes across the board. There is still time to stop, to unplug the machine, and unclip our caps, to return to words...

But Sibusiso just smiles and nods.

I flip the switch on to 'export' and wait. For me, I feel nothing. All I can do is think calming thoughts about surf rolling across Durban North beach, which should hopefully hide my more intimate thoughts. At the same time I concentrate on sending him positive thoughts that should hopefully pulse along these wires with a mood of optimism and change.

His eyes are closed and his face twists with amusement, concern, a bit of disgust, sadness... joy? I struggle to read the fast flash of feelings as they wash over his face like the sea – his mouth open, as if gasping for breath, but no sound emerges.

Silence...

I catch flashes of fire in my head, smoke stings my eyes and I fall as something hits me on the head. Glazed, I look up to see a white policeman swinging his *sjambok*.

Dogs are barking nearby, big dogs. Wetness drips down my face and my clothes are damp. I look around the shack-ridden dirtied landscape. There are hundreds of us, but hemmed in, milling, the Peace March broken as gas infiltrates our lungs and purple spray marks us as enemies of the State.

I cough and switch the machine off. Shit man, a bit of resurgent identity feedback, despite the one-way setting? I'm scared too of what Sibusiso may find, afraid of the effects of mixing brain waves, merging identities, even though our huge differences are mapped onto our skins.

Sibusiso opens his eyes and looks at me, smiling peculiarly in what looks for a moment like self-recognition.

"Well?" I ask.

"You're mostly okay, Doctor – a little more racist than you think, but a little less racist than I… worried."

"*Ag* thanks," I say. "Who's the one in need of help here, hey?

"I am sorry," he looks down, "I did not mean to be rude." (But he continues to grin.)

Someone knocks; his or her shadow filling the frosty door pane. I scrabble to pack the Box away under the desk. But it is too late. They don't wait for a reply, opening the door with only the briefest of pauses.

It's Doctor Ronald James of course, today wearing a tweed suit and sticky-looking brown tie, sparse grey hair sleeked back. He looks past Sibusiso as if he were invisible.

"Is that what I think it is, Martin?"

I've always been a poor liar, so I don't even try.

Slowly, Dr. James shakes his head: "I'm sorry, Martin, but this time you've gone too far."

"I'm busy in a therapeutic session, Doctor." There are boundaries that should be respected, whoever you are.

"This is a step too far, Martin!" He continues without blinking: "And I may have to report you for this."

I hesitate; he has good connections with the National Psychology Board.

"You will stop this session right now." Dr. James stands as my father used to; back stiff with righteousness. I know the good doctor has connections with all the training Universities too – and some whisper even more than that, retaining his active military service.

I look at Sibusiso, who returns my gaze with weary resignation, as if used to being ignored.

No, I will not reinforce this experience for him, this experience of being no one.

Dr. James is indeed a well-connected man. But then, when I was much younger, for many years I'd thought my father was directly connected to God as he claimed.

I stand, restraining an urge to swear (not in front of my patients): "Didn't you read my 'do not disturb' sign, Dr. James? Or doesn't it matter to you, because my patient is black?"

"How dare you!" He snaps, hanging on the door-handle. I refuse to sit and our gazes lock.

His eyes narrow: "On your own head be it, then." The door closes with a forceful bang, just short of slamming. Do the ghosts of one's parents never disappear, even though they have yet to die?

Sibusiso looks at me: "Trouble, Doctor?"

I smile at his leaking concern. "I think I can talk Dr. James around when I show him this machine really works. It – it does, doesn't it?"

"Yes, Doctor," Sibusiso smiles widely. "Oh yes, it works. It is blurred, not perfect, but I think it works."

"So now I can hook you up?"

Slowly, he shakes his head: "Sorry, Doctor, there is too much and too many we must protect, I can't have anyone – even you – digging around in my thoughts. It won't be safe for you either, to know what I know. And Doctor…"

"Call me Martin," I say.

He fails to even blink, all serious and stern: "And Doctor… You must also take much care the Special Branch does not get hold of this. Such a box is both wonderful and dangerous."

Ah, of course… the State secret police. I'd never thought of that. For me, it was a box to share intimacy across physical boundaries… but what about risky secrets? How do I ensure their protection too? And will they welcome a Box that reaches across the racial divide? I doubt it.

Sibusiso presses on through my thoughts: "I'm just happy to talk now and please, I also want yours and Jabu's help speaking with my father, before I'm discharged. Will I see you again tomorrow?"

Jabu is the lead male Zulu nurse, a no-nonsense man of brisk commands. I nod at Sibusiso and stand. Sibusiso takes on an aggressive political establishment; but struggles in fear with his own father... In that we share something too.

He holds a hand out and smiles as I shake it firmly. "*Hayi,* but you do need to find another woman, Doctor."

I almost snatch my hand back in shock. "That's confidential, Sibusiso."

"Sure, I know what that means. I will keep it safe, as well as my thoughts that you also smell bad."

I feel my ears redden: "See you tomorrow same time, Sibusiso."

"*Sala kahle,* stay well, Martin," he leaves quietly, gently.

The Feelings Box has been scrambled under the table. I will pack it for home at the end of the day. When to speak to Dr. James? Perhaps a day is needed to enable us both to calm down. For now, there are other patients, a pre-discharge group and ward rounds. Always work to be done here.

There is a faint whisper. I look around the room, puzzled, wondering whether it's sound reverberating from the wards through the pasty-yellow thin walls. There it is again.

I place my left ear against the cool, slightly damp wall and a word echoes through my head: "Beware, 'ware, 'ware..."

Hell, does this mean I've now got tinnitus to add to the woes of my fat and ageing body?

I laugh, but the word stays with me throughout the day, impossible to shake, whatever I do.

Voices...

"Beware, 'ware, 'ware..." the word throbs alongside alarm beeps, as I punch in the alarm de-triggering code into the pad inside the front door.

The house is quiet, the hall and dining room settled, undisturbed. I place my bag with the EE machine quietly under the dining room table.

Something's wrong. Jacky hasn't run to greet me.

I pick up an old hockey stick I keep there, just in case. Where's Jacky? The dog walker should have brought her back hours ago.

Removing my shoes, I stalk through to the kitchen; stick raised over my right shoulder.

There's a man standing by the kettle, helping himself to a cup of rooibos tea. A large black briefcase – obviously his – stands on the kitchen desktop.

He turns as I enter, with a welcoming smile that chills the muggy air.

"Good afternoon to you, Dr. Van Deventer."

Relief and then anger floods me after the initial shock of seeing him – he's white with mild blond hair, receding and lean in build, but respectfully dressed in a suit – so he's not out to rob or attack me then. I let the bottom part of the stick drop to the floor, but keep a grip on its handle with my right hand.

"Who the hell are you and where's my dog?"

He replies in Afrikaans: "My name is Brand. That's all you need to know, Doctor. I am here in the interests of the security of our country."

Ag, kak...

I drop the stick with a rattle on the tiles and look past him, but I speak Afrikaans too, knowing he sets the agenda here: "Where's my dog?"

"I shut him out the back. He wasn't very nice to me."

Yelps come from the back yard, but I leave Jacky there, suddenly too frightened to turn my back on this man.

"How the hell did you get in?" I want to step up the force of my language, but am too terrified.

"Just a few quiet words with a patriotic dog walker," he smiles.

"What do you want?"

"Your special box, Doctor – I just want that box."

I know better than to argue. White skin is not an absolute charm against harm, even in this country.

He follows me through to the lounge with his tea and briefcase. I pull the EE machine from my bag, place it on the floor, box, wires and scalp caps. He stands, assesses it calmly and takes a sip of tea.

"This is the sole prototype isn't it?" He doesn't wait for an answer, as if he knows it all already. "Well, as long as the State is the sole possessor of this box I think we can reach an agreement, Doctor. We'll be nationalising this invention solely for state purposes... in true communist fashion." He smiles again. "I trust you note the irony?

You'll need to sign this away to us – on pain of... assertive state retribution, shall we say?"

"But – but, it could help us all reach out, understand each other better; live together better, move towards peace..."

He puts his cup down on the table and looks at me. "*Fok* peace! They've declared war, or haven't you noticed, Doctor? You're betraying your own *volk* with this, don't you understand, you're a *verraier*? These are terrorists we're dealing with – and there can be no peace with terror."

I look down at the black Box. It's small, a foot square, but responsible for that magical wash of empathic feelings across Sibusiso's face earlier in the day and I feel the burn of a blow across my head.

"If you sign this box away and promise never to build another, you will be safe, my friend. We will have a similar agreement with your colleague Dr. Dan Botha."

I am no friend of his, but nor am I a hero; I look at the man's cold green eyes and am afraid, very afraid.

"All right," I say.

He wishes to seem a good-humoured man, smiling again as he hauls a sheaf of papers out of his suit pocket. He places them down on the table in front of me: "See, Doctor, we work within the rule of law, that's what makes us civilised."

I scan the terse document quickly; it's as he says, with President Terreblanche or a proxy ratifying it, so I sign in coloured triplicate. How on Earth did they find out?

"Your copy, Doctor," he hands me the green copy at the bottom.

I fold the document and put it in my trouser pocket, holding in a sudden urge to wet myself as I realise what I have to do.

Brand bends down to scoop the electro-encephalo-caps into his expandable briefcase. He has black leather gloves on now and I notice he is balding on top.

I brace myself, remembering the urgency of Sibusiso's plea; his fear. I step forward and stomp on the box, my weight crumpling its thin metallic frame with a crunching grind of broken parts. I wince as a piece of glass snags my ankle and I pull my foot back, blood starting to drip through my grey sock.

Brand lurches forward, pushing me away with a snarl on his face and I fall to the floor, clutching my ankle. He stands over me, looking down. I lie on my back and hold my right ankle, waiting for him to do something terrible.

But he doesn't.

Instead, he sits down gracefully on the floor next to me, sweeping a few shards of the broken box away with his gloved right hand.

"A mistake, Doctor, but we all make mistakes."

Why does he put himself at my level?

"I do what I do to help people like you, Doctor, but I sense you will not build us another one."

I see the calm sincerity in his face and it hits me: he is a people-reader too.

"It is no matter. You will build no more for anyone." He smiles again, but it is tinged with... sadness? "We are not so far apart, brother, we both have faith in what we do. But now that America has elected a *kaffir* president who seeks world peace and the *fokking* Nobel Peace Prize by talking down the Soviet Generals, we are losing the support we once had under the

Bushes and Blair. Now is the time we need to be strong."

I let go of my foot and sit up, bracing myself with my hands. Where is this lecture leading?

He sighs and takes something out of his top pocket, placing it on the floor-space between us: "Just doing my job, Doctor, as you do – there shall be no more feeling machines. Let this serve as a warning."

He levers himself to stand over me in one deft motion; he's fit too, a lot fitter than me.

Looking down, he repeats himself, even though I have no doubt as to his message:

"No more Feelings Boxes, Doctor van Deventer, you understand?"

Jacky's frantic yelps outside are rising in volume; she is scrabbling desperately at the door, which judders duh-duh-duh against the lock. I am aware that Brand has gone and I did not even hear him leave. I stare at what he has left me, propped up on the floor amongst the debris of my broken EE machine.

It's standing on its own rounded base, metallic, long and pointed – an unmarked rifle bullet.

It sucks in my gaze like a black hole.

I start to shiver, despite the balminess of the late summer afternoon. No, I will not stay sitting here. My bloody right foot is marked only by a shallow gash, already coagulating. I keep my sock pulled down to avoid it drying against the wound and stand up, making my way to the backdoor.

Jacky jumps into my arms. She's unhurt. Box or no box, I know she will always love me… I cuddle her on the couch and she licks my face, until I stop shivering.

The sun blazes lower and warms my face too. No point staying here.

I stand up and sweep the EE machine into the corner of the room, piece upon broken piece; springs, coils, relays, software boards… and it feels as if I'm sweeping myself raw inside. Dan will be devastated.

A double-edged sword of invention, the box now resembles little more than a broken down metal and glass toy constructor set. I'd loved construction sets as a child, but my ultimate game had been building racing tracks for electric cars, especially the trickiest part, the bridge in a figure eight. It needed just the right amount of pressure and angling... The stress of a raised bridge could mean poorly connected track-pieces and cars failing to make it over the hill.

I move to the bedroom to clean and bandage my ankle.

Suzette looks at me from the picture at my bedside, the Umgeni Bridge dangling dangerously in the background. I'd proposed marriage to her there, almost dashing across the bridge to the other side to celebrate – or perhaps show off – when she'd said 'yes'.

I remember getting some way across, but the bridge started to swing in the building breeze, alarming us both. I'd scrambled back, without pausing to help Suzette, carrying an irrational but private and enduring shame.

We never spoke about it – even though we were both psychologists in training – and a little more than seven years later, all our words ran out.

Funny thing is I'm not looking at her. Instead, I watch the thin brown rope bridge spin across the gorge, wondering how it might feel to cross that bridge now.

I am grateful that the drive through the peaceful white suburbs of Howick is quiet.

The journey grows ever quieter as I head up the valley past sweeping imported eucalyptus trees; no drifting teargas smoke to worry about, no burning tires or police blocks strewn across the road.

The mid-summer sun still hangs low with some warmth as it drops towards the hilly horizon. Christmas 2014 is nearing fast. Elections next year, but everyone knows the AWB will win hands down; De Klerk is still in prison for trying to dismantle apartheid from the inside and Terreblanche carefully ensures the safety of all ballot boxes.

It's too quiet here – I look in the rear-view mirror, but there is no car following.

I start to tap the steering wheel of my old Ford as my CDs run through their loop, especially when Aretha asks for respect, but keep glancing in my rear view mirror at the empty road behind me. (I must look up Gil Scott-Heron on Wikipedia; see if it's accessible through the State Firewalls.)

There are only a few cars left in the car parks at the entrance to the Umgeni River Valley Nature Park and I pay my way in, eyeing the 'Slegs blankes/Whites only' sign on the wooden kiosk.

My camera bounces against my chest as I wind through wooded thornveld; a few large birds shriek in the canopy. (We still wait for cam-phones, but they remain banned as a potentially easy source of troubling video.) The path drops down towards the valley and I take the detour left to where the old rope bridge used to be. It's a balmy evening and there's no one else around at this late hour. The path levels out in front of me and the bridge comes into view, but it's different from how I remember; built of strutted wood and more solid looking.

The river rumbles with summer rains below me and I smell the dung of a large mammal in the bushes near the bridge. I smell my own sweat too, as I pant to catch my breath.

Well, here it is; the swaying bridge I have never crossed.

I stand at the spot where I took those pictures almost a decade ago: one devoid of any person, fit to adorn the wall of my then new job, freshly qualified as I was. The other picture still sits as I left it beside my bed, with Suzette looking out at me; the bridge small, the valley obscured behind her long blowing brown hair.

Strange, but Suzette's face dims even more in my memory as I stand here.

The valley sweeps down towards the racing river in a torrent of brownish grass and green woodland. I take a hold of the wooden railing and step onto the struts of the bridge. They creak with my weight. I wait for a few moments and then step deliberately across, one slat at a time, focusing on the next slat, not looking over the railing.

The other side arrives almost too suddenly, my feet squelching onto damp tussocks. I hold the bridge post and swing around to check the view.

It's very similar to the other side, thicker riverine trees and bushes dropping to the edge of the rock-strewn white spraying river. But on this side there's a scarred and stripped patch I hadn't noticed down near the riverside. It's a blackened, burnt area, flat and empty, but glinting with one or two long and shiny corrugated aluminium boards lying derelict. The vegetation has not re-grown; it's fairly recent. Probably the detritus left by illegal black squatters who sneaked through the fence and set up camp before being forcibly evicted, their homes crushed, the place emptied and burnt.

Pain thumps in my head, a *sjambok*-blow pain and there's an acrid burning smell in my nose, stinging my eyes – smoke; or tear gas? Then, just as suddenly, it's gone.

I take a picture of the scorched, desolate earth. There's only one cause of fire at this time of year.

I step back onto the bridge and make my way across to the swaying middle; bracing myself as I stop to look down. I'm giddy with the deep drop to white-green water below and the pungent vegetation scented warm wind that buffets the bridge.

I cannot take a picture here; I am too afraid that I – or my camera – will topple over. Instead, I hold onto the rope railing with one hand and feel in my right pocket with the other. Bracing my feet and ignoring the burn in my strapped right ankle, I swing my right arm around and launch the grasped bullet downwind.

It spins and drops, glinting once, and I don't even see where it splashes.

I am tired of threats and ghosts.

The river rolls on and I watch, caught in its hissing motion.

I will clear my weekend of patients and go to those meetings of radical psychologists and social workers who fight for political change, saying there's no normality in an abnormal society... Ah, and I'm not a complete altruist, true – there's a good few woman psychologists and social workers who go there too, I believe.

A gust of wind rocks the bridge, pumping my heart as I stand over the Umgeni River. I hold on tighter to the railing with both hands. I need to have a word with that Dr. James too... A firm word, a *vuurwarm* word.

The bridge swings again in a gust of strong wind and I inch my way across to the car park side of the river. No point in false heroics; in any case, no one's here to see them.

On firm ground once more, I look back across the view that is captured within the pictures in my office and bedroom. No, this is definitely a different bridge, a newer bridge. It doesn't look nearly as far across to the other side anymore either. Perhaps it's my new perspective – but I also have a sense that maybe most of the vastness of the chasm has been inside my head.

Brand has called me both a brother and a traitor to my people. But I don't know who 'my people' are anymore.

There is no one else standing by the bridge. Suzette is gone.

I walk back up the sloping path, glancing ahead. On the distant hill summit above me, I see the long rocking neck of a giraffe. It's blackly silhouetted in solitude, near a bent thorn tree against the fading sky. Giraffes are social animals; I know there must be other members of the herd on the far side of the hill, but still I feel a pang of empathic loneliness.

I have heard rumours the South African Defence Force have been here too, poaching ivory to fund our local War on Terror. Would they target a bit of family giraffe meat?

I am too afraid to climb the hill, for fear there is nothing on the other side.

Stay focused, stay here: It'll be good to see Sibusiso tomorrow. And I mustn't neglect to help him sort out his relationship with his father before discharge, as the ward closes briefly for the year's end.

Perhaps it's time I speak to my own father again...

Something howls in the bush to my left and I break into a wincing jog uphill.

No silence here, but the wild languages remain alien to me.

Still, it's good to hear voices.

I pant up the path as I head back to the car-park and realise I am rebuilding the EE machine in my head, piece by bloody piece... and not for the State either. Why?

What can I say?

I build bridges.

Chapter 5
Sibusiso's Beast

Today, the white doctor turns up with his black box.

My stomach grows heavier as he places the box carefully on the desk between us.

"Look, Sibusiso." He shows me two sets of leads coming out of the box from either side, "These are the leads which connect our brains together so that we can communicate – you know, talk – without words."

I know what 'communicate' is – I study to teach history and geography in English at *Fundimiso* College. Or I did once, before...

He continues to talk slowly, as if to match my brain.

"Of course it's a new invention and so I need you to sign you're happy with trying it out." I want to laugh, because Dumisani told me they asked for his 'X' when it came to shocking his brain to make him better. He refused, but still they did it, *in his best interests.*

I do not laugh though; I can see the doctor is serious.

And excited: "See here, this switch changes the directional flow of the brain-waves between us so we can change who reads whose mind at any one time."

Ah, it is a good toy, but one that makes me even more ill.

He notices my face. "Sibusiso, what's wrong?"

Give him his due, he does not call me Edward, my European label from them – and his pronunciation is passable. I look around the small yellow-green room with no windows. I see no cameras or listening devices, but they may still be there, tiny, hidden and waiting to bite.

"You're not going to connect that to my genitalia are you, Doctor van Deventer?" I ask.

His hands freeze across the dials and switches littering his box. "*Liewe God*, of course not, what do you think this is?"

He does not ask me how I know a word such as 'genitalia'; so I wait for the *cents* to drop.

"*Ag* no man, Sibusiso, we're here to help you, this is not some sort of torture thing – can you tell me where you are?"

I sigh, it's a question I have been asked many times and to the point I have grown to doubt my answer: "Fort Napier Psychiatric Hospital."

"Good," he smiles with encouragement. "And what's the date today?"

I am not an old man with a fading brain. I stand, with a fist of hot feeling thrusting up my spine.

He steps back, glancing at the closed door behind him. "Uh... Sibusiso?"

"Friday, December 8th."

"Oh, uh, *ja* right, um well, are you ready to be hooked up to the machine?"

I continue to stand as I see it unsettles him - and he has no taser-prod in his hand. "No."

He looks disappointed: "We went through this yesterday and I thought you'd agreed, why not now?"

"There are things in my mind that are precious to me. Why..." It is hard to ask a question of a white man.

But I have to, for the sake of Bongani from my college, now three days in a *boere* cell, for the sake of dead Mandla. "Why are my words alone not enough? And..." This is a harder question still, so I clench my fists and swallow, to force it through: "Why should I trust you, Doctor?"

"Ahh..." he relaxes then, as if it had only just occurred to him: "Listen Sibusiso, I am not connected to the Security Police at all. In fact..." This time he looks around the room and I can see some small doubt and fear on his face: "I'm on the run from the Military Police, as I have refused to serve in the army. Thankfully they haven't chased me hard, as they're too busy dealing with unrest in the townships."

Thankfully! My throat chokes on that word. So many of my brothers and sisters are dying out there in the '*unrest*'?

He sees my face. "I'm sorry Sibusiso, I didn't mean to offend you and it was a stupid, selfish thing to say." He nods his head in apology. Why does he *need* his box? It looks like he is not such a bad reader of my expressions, after all.

He gestures towards the machine. Ah, it is a toy that smells both of his sweat *and* his ambition.

I sit, but I will not be meek. "Two conditions, Doctor."

He grinds into his chair, wobbling a little with excitement. "What are they, Sibusiso?"

I stop as the wave of feelings that brought me here sweep over me again. They squeeze my words dry with hollow emptiness, freezing my brain with thoughts of death. In the end, that's all there is. Nothing else survives.

A man waves his hands in my face, but those hands will wither and fade; the fat man will become a skeleton and the wind on my cheeks will go.

He is pulling me up from my chair, holding my hands, massaging my arms, getting me to move, to step around that small room. "Come on, man!" he barks.

He is not afraid to touch me. Other lighter feelings swing into my arms and head. He is not afraid to touch me. That's *kakhulu* good for a white man. My head and throat thaws, just like an early spring stream high up on the *Ukhahlamba* Mountains, where I often long to go.

"Enough, Doctor."

He smiles at me: "Feeling a bit better, Sibusiso?"

"Surely," I say.

"Would you rather leave it then? Shall we end our session now?"

I look down at him; he is a short man, but his face is near mine, there is no longer a desk between us. I can see and smell his sweat; bursting through a sickly sweet smell he must layer over himself daily like concrete.

"Two conditions," I say, "One, this is never shared with the *SB*." He knows of whom I speak, there are no worse devils than those from the Special Branch. "Two, I get to read you first."

He steps back in surprise. "*Ja* man, of course to the first one, but your second condition is a little less – uh – orthodox."

He notices my look: "Unusual."

There is nothing wrong with unusual. Unusual is good.

He seems less sure. "Okay…" he says with reluctance, seemingly only agreeing due to the lure of his machine.

I sit and wait while he clips a pad of funny stuff on my head, struggling a bit with only short tufts to anchor the clips, it's still less than a week after my admissions shave. His hair is much easier; he must go to a nice barber, he gets the netting clips to dangle against his scalp.

He looks at me over the box and I see he is sweating even more. "Ready, Sibusiso?"

I nod with a warning glare that lets him know he must do this right. If I have any sense he is reading me, I will tear this tissue from my head and stay mute with him.

He flicks a switch and I wait.

Nothing.

Or, as the *boere* say, *fok* all!

Then I hear it, like my father's fuzzy radio high up in the mountains, where we used to slow twist the dials to edge a faint voice from the roar of static, searching for Radio Freedom. This machine hisses too, a 'shhhhh' of sound like a distant waterfall, but there are no dials I can twist. The doctor watches me with a blank look and fiddles with his machine.

Is that a faint voice I hear, a deeper rumble amongst the hiss? I strain my ears but the sounds are inside me. Is that a name – Parton; Martin? The rumble and hiss warm me but there's an ice-prick of loneliness and desire, hidden by thoughts of… standing up on an ironing board, riding sea-waves?

I look up at him in puzzlement and he switches the machine off. "Well," he says, "Does it work, Sibusiso?"

"Perhaps."

"What do you mean? What was I thinking then?"

"That your first name is Martin and you need a woman."

"Yes!" he shouts and clenches his fists in front of his face: "My name is indeed Martin and I've been divorced for a few years now!"

I wish I could join his joy, but perhaps someone on the ward mentioned his first name and he just *looks* lonely to me? I want to ask about the board but stop; I've seen pictures of mad white men riding waves on boards in the magazines we cut up for art therapy.

I do not wish to cast doubt on his joy. For although I am young, I know real happiness is rare, perhaps even for an *umlungu*.

"You can have a turn tomorrow," he smiles at me.

There is a knock at the door and he scrambles to hide his machine away, shoving it under the desk.

But the door is already open and an old pale man looks in. I have seen the old man walk into our ward a few times, swinging his arms freely, as if he has great power.

"Is that what I think it is, Martin?"

My doctor looks frightened. The old man shakes his head: "I'm sorry, Martin, this time you've gone too far."

So a man scolds a boy. Does the old man wish to protect what is inside my head?

"I'm busy in a therapeutic session, Doctor!" There is more steel in the younger doctor's voice.

The old man is not impressed and shakes his head: "I will report you for this. You will stop this session right now!"

Dr. van Deventer looks at me with a peculiar expression that is hard to read. He stands abruptly: "Did you not read my 'do not disturb' sign, Dr. James? Or does it not matter to you, because my patient is black?"

"How *dare* you!" The old man barks with teeth in his voice: "On your own head be it, then."

The door slams, the sound shaking me.

"Trouble, Doctor?" I ask.

"I think I can talk him round," he says, "The box, the Empathy Enhancer does work doesn't it, Sibusiso?"

"Yes, Doctor," I say, knowing they are the words he wants to hear. I keep my face calm, but it is a strange thought that even the *umlungu* fight amongst themselves.

"See you tomorrow then, Sibusiso?"

I smile, but am not so sure.

Tonight, I ask for curry.

The coloured woman behind the counter pauses and looks me up and down as if I smell bad. "You're only allowed *Bantu* food."

I look at the *samp* and beans. They have been so over-cooked and mixed; it's as if they have passed through someone's irritable bowels.

The dark feelings drop on me again, threatening to smother me. I think of dead Mandla and hold my plate out: "I want curry."

She lifts the large metal spoon as if she wants to strike me. I see a security man move forwards from a corner of the dining hall, brown uniform bursting with eagerness. I put my plate down extravagantly with one hand, before leaving the piss-yellow hall, now starting to throng and seethe with hungry people.

It is but a few paces to the ward, along the darkened path. I am not *so* mad; my ward, at least, is 'open'. *Jabula* Ward they call it, although I feel no joy here.

Jabu, Chief Nurse Nhlapo, looks at me in surprise. He is sorting out piles of brightly coloured pills.

"You're back early, Sibusiso. You ate quickly."

I do not disabuse him of the idea. He holds out a pink pill. "You might as well have yours now, then."

I fist the pill and he gives me a glass of water, watching as I swallow water and air.

"Good," he turns back to his piles, but with a buck-shy

curious look at me, as if he wonders what I am thinking. His quick, precise movements remind me of my dead mother. He is a big man, neatly dressed in his uniform, sleeves buttoned primly down around his wrists.

I don't know if he is safe to talk to. I don't know who masters his politics.

I walk down the corridor, between galleys of dishevelled bunks and find my own bed. It's nestled in the far corner, the furthest I could find; although I pay at night with a farter in the bunk above me.

The ward is quiet now though, all are out to eat.

The doctor awaits me with his thought box tomorrow. I am hungry and the crushing blackness, like a beast inside me, hangs on the edge of my vision. I sit on thin, creaking mattress springs and think.

Father.

I know better than to go home; if Bongani talks, it will not be safe for my family. Shall I wait instead? Shall I give this Doctor Martin Van Deventer and his magic box a chance to drive these demons away?

The darkness is seeping inside me, locking my bones with its cruel grip, like a mamba's bite. It will be so easy just to lie back and wait for it to slowly suffocate me. *Izinto zabantu, who* bewitches me?

So easy just to lie back...

But my father never lay back; he still works his head and hands as a cattle-herd for baas Esterhuyze and a tax clerk for the *induna,* to feed all of us. "My turn to be looked after will come," he used to remind us pointedly.

Father!

I stand somehow with gritted teeth. I rub my arms and legs, thrusting blood into them, like the doctor had done for me this morning. I need to move.

The darkness is a beast, tearing at my insides, but I ignore it. A feeling from the morning's box floats into me.

Alone; cut off; dead. Loneliness.

Are they the doctor's or are they mine?

In the end, does it matter? As for now, I need to keep moving.

I need to get away.

I pull my rucksack with difficulty from under the bunk. I will leave. The back door is open, as is the gate for walkers into the world, just a few curves of a dimly-lit path around past the dining hall.

I've traced the route many times, only to stop short of the boomed gate, wondering: where shall I go? I know of no safe houses nearby. Outside, the world burns and the army and police kill us without thought. So it was for Mandla - and his brother. I have no wish to die, whatever this beast within me may say.

This room at least is safe. Am I a coward?

"What are you doing?"

It is Chief Nurse Nhlapo, standing at the opposite end of the dormitory, watching me with my slung back-pack, standing near the back-door.

What can I say?

He looks angry for a minute and then his face softens. "Come talk to me, my boy. I can't stop you going, they have not certified you, but it is your family who brought you here for your own good. I will be in the Station." He gestures towards himself expansively and then leaves.

My soul flares with excitement. Nurse Nhlapo's large beckoning movement shrugs his sleeve ever-so-slightly from his thick right forearm. Underneath, I catch a glimpse of a hidden braided leather bracelet with black, green and gold beads. He turns and hitches his sleeves down in one fluid and muscular motion.

I know now who masters his politics – and the Nurses' Station is indeed private.

I put the rucksack back under my bunk and reach inside the front pocket of my blue hospital dungarees. I pull out a sticky samosa I'd grabbed earlier with my left hand when placing the plate down flamboyantly with my right, distracting that witch behind the counter.

I take a spicy bite and walk towards the Nurses' Station. I *will* talk with the Chief Nurse of *umlungus* with magic thinking boxes, of canteen food and the pills he sorts so carefully for all of us.

And next time I will *insist* on the curry.

The doctor cancels our appointment, saying he will see me next week. He gives no reason, so my thoughts about him darken.

Still, three days with Jabu, whispering together when moments allow us, does wonders for me, easing the bite of the Beast within.

Saturday is here.

Bongani is out; the police have let him free, he texts me, saying he has said nothing. He comes to fetch me for the weekend, but he is late, so I am already packed and ready to go with Nombuso.

As usual, he walks in tentatively through the ward door, as if fearing to be attacked by a horde of madmen. I jump at him snarling and he shrieks and steps back into the door slamming shut behind him.

"Ow!– What the fuck, Sib?"

There is a guttural roll of laughter behind me – there is little femininity about Nombuso's behaviour, but I don't mind.

Bongani notices the backpack hanging off my shoulders: "You ready to roll, brother?"

Nombuso steps alongside me: "He's coming with me this weekend."

Bongani eyes her warily: "But Sib always comes back to the college on weekends."

I tire of people talking about me as if I were not there.

"I'm going with Nombuso today, Bongani," I shiver as Nombuso slips her arm through mine. "Sorry *bra*, I couldn't tell you in time to save you the trip – she just turned up a few minutes ago and… persuaded me. I don't think college is safe anymore."

He scowls: "I wonder how she persuaded you, hey?"

I feel my face burn a bit at his suggestion, but Nombuso only laughs: "You must come up and visit us, 'gani, I'll text you the address." He scowls. It seems he does not like the way she shortens names – or takes control.

Nombuso pulls me past him, "Come on, Sib, I've got something to show you."

Outside, parked in the Medical Superintendent's bay, squeezed alongside his black Merc, is a motorbike; a dilapidated 250cc Japanese bike.

Two helmets hang off the front bars. "No need to lock it, hey – not many *tsotis* wonder into a lunatic asylum looking for stuff to steal!"

She drives that bike like she belongs with me in Fort Napier!

I hang onto her, sweating, oblivious to the nearness of her body, as she accelerates and bends over into the road corners. She is helmeted in black so no one knows she is black as she throttles past a yellow police van. It feels as if she is flirting dangerously with them, the road and the speed limit.

She circles around town and then sweeps up a hill, with what looks like a set of neat houses off to the right. I see an Indian man walking towards one of the houses, so I assume it's the Indian area of town.

Nombuso takes a sudden sharp bend to the right and we drop down a dirt slope towards the base of a hill. Off to our left are sprawls of half-drowned trees, branches straining above a lake that must have pooled from the summer rains.

In front of us is another hill, but blunted, with rock exposed and rubble at the base. White stone, almost like the limestone quarry on Robben Island, where it is rumoured Mandela has died. No one has confirmed this though, the government no doubt aware the country would boil, if this were so.

Nombuso just revs her bike like an aggressive lion and surges up the bumping dirt-track curving to our left, past the lake and up past village huts perched above, cattle fields emerging to our right.

Nombuso stands up to avoid the rat-tat-tat of the broken road thumping up through the seat, but I am too scared to do so. Instead, I groan at the ache in my balls.

As the ground levels out, she brings the bike to a gravelly dusty halt and my face rams into her back.

She kicks the bike stand down and I gratefully drop my feet onto solid ground. She sits and turns her head; our helmets knock with a hollow clunk. She lifts her visor.

"You've got to get off first, 'Biso. I can't swing my legs over the bars in front."

I nod, clunking my chin with the helmet, tasting the salty iron sting of blood in my mouth from banging my helmeted face in her back – Nombuso herself barely flinched.

Silly to nod in this thing, so I undo the strap, pull off the helmet and swing my leg over the back of the bike onto glorious solid ground. Nombuso swings her body off the bike with practiced ease, removes her helmet and shakes her near-bald head, as if in memory of what hair she may once have had.

She's stocky, straight faced and plain, but I feel a twinge in my crotch - she fills out her leather jacket *very* well.

"Welcome to Hope's Folly," she gestures to her left.

Behind a white and yellow frangipani tree slinks a long low dull white building with a faded green corrugated roof. The bzzzz noise focuses my gaze on a hornet's nest, hanging over the nearest window.

Angled off to the left behind the building is a small outhouse and a *rondawel*, neatly circular, but white brick, not mud. To the right of the building a towering red bougainvillea drapes forward over wooden struts on a *stoep*, a wide verandah space gazing down into the valley.

Nombuso gives a mock bow: "Welcome to Cell Hartebeest

of MK. You have to come in now, 'Biso," she laughs and swings her helmet in front of her: "Else we might have to kill you."

Umkhonto we Sizwe! Mandela's armed wing of the ANC. I must have stepped backwards, because I almost trip over the bike's stand arm.

Nombuso doubles over with laughter: "it's just a joke, 'Biso – man, you can be too serious. Come inside and I'll introduce you to the others."

She saunters off to what looks like the back door behind the building, without looking back.

I am aware of the tingling in my crotch becoming a throb, but my father always warned me against listening to my cock too much. I hesitate, knowing if I go inside that building, there is indeed no going back.

Not only were MK most definitely banned – as the armed wing of the ANC they were most actively sought by the *boere* – police, military, Special Branch, the whole fucking – (inwardly I wince, Father would not approve the word, but it fits) – lot of the aggressive white forces.

The ones who killed Mandla.

I close my eyes, too frightened to move. Inside me, I sense the Beast pacing, a vague dark shape of fury, snarling and ready to rip at my innards.

I am tired of this.

Come on then, I shout, readying myself in my mind, *what are you waiting for?*

The Beast needs no further goading and leaps suddenly, almost taking me by surprise.

Almost.

My mind-self drops onto my right knee and the black shape soars over me, but my hands have arced a mental loop around its neck. I straighten and brace my legs, hands twined around my mind-leash. The Beast almost rips the leash from my grasp and rears up, roaring, spinning to smack me with its huge paw, but I have lent backwards and it meets only air. Hot saliva spatters off my face.

The Beast crouches, growling, but hesitant suddenly, as if aware of the taut band around its throat.

I tighten the grip of my right hand. It's a choke chain and I have the will to wield it.

The Beast slowly subsides to the ground.

It's one fucking huge Black Panther.

I open my eyes.

Nombuso is watching me from the window under the hornet's nest, standing a few respectful inches back from the buzzing traffic.

"*Hayi*, 'Biso, what *are* you doing?"

"Just thinking," I say, hiding my embarrassment. But my legs feel strong now and I have no qualms about walking forwards, angling around to the open, battered back door.

I hesitate for only a moment before stepping into the cooler hallway shade of that old farmhouse, Hope's Folly.

Chapter 6
Martin Rebuilds Pandora's Box

How do you recreate a masterpiece?

I'm no engineer. As a neuropsychologist, I'm in touch with my shortcomings. I guess you do it the same way you did the first time, but this time, a hell of a lot more secretly – and with an awareness that this will have to be kept 'in-house'. Do we have the resources?

Dan will know.

So here I am, sitting outside his house in my car, night already camped in, slumped down in the front-seat so that I am unobtrusive – and feeling faintly ridiculous. I watch my rear view mirror but see no one moving in the few scattered cars parked behind me. Most people have their cars securely locked away in their garages, even though white Hilton has been kept quiet by a phalanx of army barricades. They check your Books of Life instead of your skin colour, as they used to some years back. Ruth First and Joe Slovo may have been assassinated, but their list of white terrorists is no doubt longer than they would like.

A dog barks in the distance, but it sounds bored rather than agitated. I wait for a man to walk well past with his dog before opening the door to slide out. I finger my phone, too frightened to text, in case it's hackable. Dan may be surprised – to date, we've kept our co-operation and relationship firmly within work bounds, even though we're old school friends (of sorts).

I ring the bell, heart pounding.

There is a clatter of locks and chains and I feel inspected by the peephole in the door. It is late, after nine, and I hope I haven't woken their young daughter - eight or nine if I remember correctly.

Dan opens the door, slightly bleary-eyed in a bright red dressing gown. *"Wat die fok, Martin?"*

He swings his gaze from me to the street behind me. Ah, he's been visited too, then! He waves me in with a discreet swishing of his right palm, stepping back to widen the door in order to allow me in.

I creep in sideways like a crab, backpack scraping his cream hallway wall.

Dan closes the door behind me and I think '*very* nice!'

The hallway is wide, but studded with original artwork, an incongruous mixture of local seascapes and what looks like 3-D township art, shack scenes with background rolling green Midland hills, a few shacks fore-grounded in bent metal jutting from cheap plywood. It's not the art alone that's caught my eye — the hallway drifts into the distance, with a good few rooms pegged off, both left and right. They must rattle around in here, the three of them. I wonder whether he was born into money.

Dan's pushing me through into the first room on the right and we dip down a few steps into a lushly furnished lounge - black stinkwood suite, an original-looking Persian rug splayed on what looks like a yellowwood floor.

A woman stands waiting for us as we step down. She's small, fading brown hair and a face starting to line, but her strong green eyes fail to falter as she returns my handshake squeeze with interest.

"Helen, this is Martin van Deventer, a colleague I may have mentioned. Martin, my wife Helen." Dan stands next to her and they both eye me carefully. I notice they haven't asked me to sit down.

I open my mouth, but realise I'm not sure what to say. I have remembered her much vaunted mind-reading skills from Dan's accounts and feel out-psyched.

Helen laughs and seems to visibly relax, "It's late, as I'm sure you are aware, Martin, so please don't waste time gaping like a stunned fish. You have half an hour tops, so sit down and Dan will get you a drink."

Dan leaves the room without a word.

I recall the way he slightly lowered his voice on the few occasions he briefly mentioned his wife and anxiety traipses inside me with *songololo* feet.

"Well," she snaps, "get on with it!"

I glance at the empty doorway; this seems to increase her irritation.

"Come on," she growls. "Dan's smart enough to catch up – you boys have obviously been busy!"

"Well," I say, "Perhaps you've also had a visit from a – a branch of the police."

"Ja," she says, leaning back in a chair, plucking a cigarette out of a box she's dug from the pocket of her full length, white dressing-gown, "The fuckers were here too – smoke?"

She offers a box of Zimbabwean Zest, legalized low strength *dagga*. I shake my head as she lights up. "*Ja*, don't tell me, drugs do anaesthetise the proletariat, I've heard it all before, Martin, from Dan..."

I'm relieved when Dan walks in and puts a tray of *rooibos* tea down on their squared yellowwood coffee table.

I take a sip, trying not to wrinkle my nose at the sweet puff of *dagga* smoke in the air. "Well, they wanted the – uh, *Box* Dan and I have been working on."

"Yes, your glorious Pandora's Box that Dan finally mentioned – but only *after* the police came nosing around our house, taking our computers. I'm still trying to get them back, but the rule of law is not always straightforward in this country, as you may have noticed."

She leans back and takes another deep drag; the glow on the end of the cigarette seems to have been sucked from her belly. I see now why Dan sits timidly on the arm frame of her chair, sipping quietly. He obviously told her very little up until their... visit.

"The bastards upset Jody, so I gave them the fruits of some *suiwer* Afrikaans," she goes on, eyeing the *zol* in her right hand, small expert smoke rings escaping out of the side of her mouth.

Despite myself, I smile, but Dan is leaning forward, looking worried.

"You didn't give them the Box did you, Martin?"

I shake my head; the top of my mouth feels numb; I've been sipping the hot tea too quickly.

"Is that it, in your backpack?"

I nod, feeling a little ashamed. "Sort of."

He puts his tea cup down on the table carefully: "*What* do you mean?"

I swing the bag off my back, pull it open and slowly place the box with its crushed casing on the floor. I scoop most of the components back inside its battered shell.

"What the hell happened to it?" Martin jumps to his feet to join me, stares down in disbelief at the battered box next to my feet.

"I... stood on it."

"You *what?*" He's kneeling down, stroking the box, probing the crushed metal surface.

I'm too embarrassed to speak.

After a pause of several seconds, he cranes his neck around to look up at me: "*You* did this? Jesus, Martin, you seriously need to lose some weight man."

There's a gasping, choking noise. Helen is doubled over, caught between pulling in smoke and laughing. It takes her a good minute to recover her breath, by which time Dan is back from the kitchen with a glass of water.

It wasn't *that* funny.

"Is it fixable?" I ask.

"Put it this way," he says, "this isn't an overnight job, it's not a 'Breakano' Set."

"And the specs – do the cops have those now?"

Dan taps his nose. "I deleted the sensitive records and they never found the external hard drive I loaded the red-prints on."

I feel a growing excitement: "How long, Dan?"

He shrugs. "If I call in a few favours from *tekkies* I know in

Jo'burg, I'd say a week at the outside."

Helen squeezes a last drag out of her cigarette and angrily stubs it out in a saucer before Dan manages to pick up the tray. "Dan, dear,' she says sweetly.

He lifts the tray and I hear the cups rattle, but his voice is steady: "Yes, dear?"

"If Jody gets hurt as a result of any of this, you'll be sleeping out your days on that ratty couch in your poky university office, understand?"

I catch his eye; his expression is hard and determined "Yes, dear," he says, exiting the room, tray in hand. This time, the crockery doesn't shift an inch.

Helen's eyes lose focus and she gazes into the distance, smiling to herself. I'm starting to feel light-headed, so I wander over to the window and peer discreetly through the gap in the curtains out into the road.

"Who are you and what you want?" A little girl is standing in the doorway, clutching a teddy bear aggressively under her left arm, her brown hair tousled from sleep.

Helen jerks out of her daze, swiftly walks over to her: "Just a friend of Daddy's who's about to leave, darling, let's go back to bed now, shall we?"

The mother models bluntness successfully for her daughter.

As Helen walks past me, she hands me a card, "Bye Martin, be careful out there. I hope you won't need this."

While I wait for Dan to return, I look down at the small plain business card, instantly recognising the name: Helen De Lange MA LLB. No wonder Dan walks on eggshells around her. She's a top-notch corporate lawyer, often quoted in the papers.

Dan may not have inherited his money after all.

He slumps back into the lounge, a grumpy expression on his face. Maybe he's just exhausted. "You on your way, Marty?"

"Yes," I say, "when the guy walking his dog gets to the bottom of the road."

He grimaces: "You've seen him too, hey? It's no wonder

Helen's so jumpy."

"A week you reckon?"

"Tops," he says, leading me to the front door. Once it's open, I make a quick dash for my car.

Somewhere in the neighbourhood, another dog barks.

They hold their meeting in a surprisingly public place, for an organization toying with a banning order. I pretend to be looking at University posters, hanging outside in the reception room of the Main Hall, Scottsville Campus, having picked up an e-mail alert about the meeting from Professor Pillay, our Principal Psychologist. Dan is in Jo'burg, supposedly fixing the EE machine with the aid of some cutting-edge software engineers.

There are lots of Afro-Rap and Cyber-Jazz concert sessions advertised, as well as people looking for accommodation, cheap psychological textbooks or orgasmic enlightenment. I am not looking too hard though, engaging my peripheral view to see who is entering the hall, keeping a particular lookout for anyone resembling Special Branch agent Brand.

Down near the right hand bottom corner of the board I see Ad Lib and The Four Horsemen are creaking out of retirement; as is an ever defiant Roger Lucey, with his Zub Zub Marauders. The killer is the opening band though – a black Afro-jazz outfit from Umlazi called The Terrorists, who have just played The Rainbow Club in Pinetown. Now that looks like it could be a lively concert, as the organisers have no doubt *not* applied for official permission.

People jostle past. Unable to stand it, I move into the hall itself, a high-ceilinged room lined with a row of chairs facing an empty mike on stage. I choose a chair on the right-hand side of the back row, pick up a small sheet lying on the chair and hold a newspaper up. I can angle and dangle the paper, looking past it, without being *too* obvious.

The seats at the front are filling up fast. Most of their occupants are youngsters of course; students are easily radicalized, despite the occasional whiff of tear-gas or thrash of a *sjambok* on a march. What surprises me is there are more females than males. Some are attractive indeed, but perhaps a bit on the young side for me. I spot our Principal Psychologist, Professor Pillay, searching for a seat near the front.

I find my newspaper dropping as the rows fill up.

A fat youngster squeezes in next to me: he's black-haired, with faded acne pockmarks and a shave shadow around his lower face and upper lip. A faded-looking but interesting brunette with short punky hair slips in next to him. She's slight and boyish, but looks to be pushing forty.

I notice she glances at my copy of the Mercury before she sits down, as if interested in finding out which page I'm on. I almost want to fold it up; she doesn't look as if she's a rugby fan. Her face is deadpan though, and when she sits down I can hardly see her around the burping bulk of the man between us. Music kicks out of the speakers - aggressive sounding *Afrikaner* music.

The big youngster shifts excitedly in his chair and turns to me, "Kerkorrel – under house arrest now you know and openly a *moffie* too..."

I grunt, suspecting he just wants to show off his knowledge. Sure enough, he turns back to watch the stage. Five people are filing up the steps, taking seats behind the mike. Two white men, two white women and one wispy looking Indian woman.

I look at the leaflet I'd almost sat on – the Indian woman must be Wadwalla – she's wearing a translucent purple scarf, perhaps she's a Muslim.

A stanza of street smart rap-kwela staccatoes into the room: the harsh biting vocals of Nick Pereira filling the space with his call for 'Burn the Barricades'.

The young man looks puzzled, so I lean across to him, "The Rude Boys."

He scowls at me.

A thickset white man with a blond moustache stands up and taps the mike, which screeches momentarily, and the buzz of conversation in the hall drops. The theme for the talks tonight is 'galvanizing social-psychological resources – for a better South Africa. '

The man starts talking. Initially, I find it hard to concentrate, wondering instead whether he'd make a good prop forward for the Banana Boys, the Natal rugby team. And, as I lean forward slightly, I catch a better side view of the woman, who is rocking forward, listening intently. She has an attractive face, high cheek-boned, a little furrow forming in-between her light brows as she concentrates.

I decide I'd better make an attempt to listen too. Who knows? Maybe we'll get a chance to compare notes.

Glancing at the sheet, I assume that the speaker must be Dr. Breedt. He's talking about the human cost in terms of victims of violence in the townships, wants health professional volunteers to mobilize in response, including white expertise.

As he finishes up, I feel the weight of someone's gaze. I turn my head, pulse speeding up when I realise the attractive woman has transferred her attention from the stage to me.

I try to keep staring forward, straining my peripheral vision, disappointment clutching at me as the woman stares forward again, no doubt in response to Ms. Wadwalla as she starts speaking.

According to the pamphlet, oh, *Doctor* Fariedah Wadwalla is a lecturer at *Fundimiso* College and there's a brief burst of applause as she thanks the organization for inviting her. A man at the front of the hall stands up to photograph her; she blinks as the flash hits her eyes.

I catch my breath. I'd recognize Brand anywhere. He rocks on his heels and scans the crowd, camera at the ready.

Swamped with panicked nausea, I lever myself carefully out of my seat, trying to screen my face with the newspaper. As I'm hunched over, trying to slide out without being noticed, the fat man next to me turns to me and says: "Are you leaving because they've got an Indian speaking?"

I resist slapping him with my paper, concentrating on weaving behind the chairs towards the door. The attractive brunette turns to give me a quizzical smile.

For just a moment, my panic eases. I fumble in my pocket and haul out my private practice card. "Call me," I hear my idiotic voice saying, as if from outside me, flipping the card over her right shoulder and into her lap.

Then I'm stepping into the hallway and out into the balmy evening, cursing myself for being so brazen. Might she be the type of woman who'd be impressed by the ornate lettering of the Ph.D. behind my name, though?

Despite my Doctorate, it takes me a good few minutes to find my car.

It took me a good while to locate the Pine Nut Motel, on the outskirts of 'Maritzburg and almost on the Comrades Marathon road to Durban. Dan had asked me to delete the text too, in case my phone got hacked, so I'd scribbled the address on the back of the Psychology Protest sheet.

I park in front of a low-slung yellow prefab-style building which, despite the flashing sign advertising free cable TV at the front, oozes cheapness. It's a cool night, the tarmac still slippery from the remnants of the late afternoon storm. The parking lot is fairly empty, but I feel uncomfortably exposed as I tread around neon-tinged shallow pools, heading for the Reception.

He'd booked in as a Mr. Smit; I wonder whether that had raised any sceptical laughter.

The glass door reinforced with squared metal grilling is heavy and stiff, requiring a shoulder leaned into it in order to push it open under squeaking protest. A large white security guard with a raggedy beard and gun hanging from a belt at maximum stretch around his waist barely glances at me as I stride past him, heading for the corridor door, as if I know exactly where I'm going.

"Hey," a man shouts from behind the reception desk, but I

pretend not to hear him.

"Oi," he shouts again; I sense the security guard waking up a bit behind me.

"Shit..." I murmur, turning with reluctance to the reception desk, with its large 'No guns/*Geen Vuurwapens*' sign hanging over the walled recess where the desk is placed. The receptionist - a thin swarthy man who looks to be on the edge of reclassification - is obviously exempt. I notice a lump on his hip, partially hidden underneath his tight brown corduroy jacket.

"Where you going, *boet?*"

"Just to visit a friend," I say, trying to appear casual.

"Who's that then, my china?"

"Uh – Mister Smit in 129."

"What?" he looks momentarily confused: "You mean to say he *smaaks ouens* too?"

"Huh?" I'm lost for a moment too and then think, Dan, you dirty dog; it's obviously not the first time you've been here.

"Just go up man, but I don't want no mess or anything sticky left behind, okay? You catch my drift?"

I do indeed.

As will Dan.

I find room 129 at the end of a dingy ill-lit greenish corridor. The hallway smells of old urine and, somewhat oddly, stale curry.

The 2 is hanging upside down, just missing concealing the security peep-hole around eye height. I knock briskly, a neon light flickering and buzzing above my head. I hear padded footsteps and glower through the peephole, although all I see is a vague dark shape shifting.

The door opens to a worried looking Dan in yellow T-shirt, faded jeans and white *takkies*. I push my way past him and into a small bedroom; a tiny en-suite toilet and shower off to the left. Apart from a lumpy bed draped in a stained coverlet, the room is empty of furniture; clearly its patrons don't come here to work.

Dan locks the door and turns the shower on full. "Seen that in a Bond movie," he confides with a smile. "No one should hear us now, if the room is bugged."

"We still have a water shortage," I point out, "And how will they have known to bug this room?"

He shrugs awkwardly and drops his eyes.

"So, shall we do it here on the bed – or do you prefer the floor?"

"What?" He stares at me as if he thinks I'm mad, but his shifting eyes and the faint pinking of his cheeks betrays some embarrassment.

"That bastard Joubert at the desk blabbing too much again – that's the last time he gets a tip from me."

"How can you do this to Helen?"

He frowns in the deepening flush of his face: "Oh come off it Martin, you couldn't even sustain your own marriage."

"Yes," I feel my own anger rising: "But at least we didn't cheat on each other."

"Who says we're built for monogamy anyway? You saw how sharp Helen was with me."

"But you fucking *let* her!"

He sighs deeply and bends down, digging a red duffle bag from under the bed. "Look, drop it okay, we're getting nowhere with this, let's just stick to why we're here."

The bed dips slightly under the weight of the bag. He pulls on the draw-string and slides the box out. The top section is brown, not black like the other five sides. He seems to read my mind, but then, we do go back a long way.

"So they couldn't match the colours, the main thing is whether it works or not – at least they seem to have made a decent stab at fixing it, although our research funds are pretty arid by now."

"Did you try it out?"

He grins, a bit too broadly, as if to smooth over our earlier disagreement, "You joking, Marty? Who wants someone else knowing their deepest darkest secrets – and we have no health guarantees on the machine. You *skim* you can get your black patient to do this again?"

Sibusiso.

I shrug. "I can try, I guess."

He packs the Box back in the bag and hands me the cords carefully. "Oh – and please take better fucking care of it this time, we can't afford any more uh, breakages."

I swing it onto my back, shrug my jacket over it. I now look like the Hunchback of Notre Dame.

Dan playfully slaps my cheeks on both sides. "This is our future fortune on your back, okay *broer*, so again, be fucking careful – I'm in the process of trade-marking and copyrighting this as our EE Machine. We can make one hell of a packet if we market this right."

I look at him aghast: "I thought this was to advance human communication and connection and the science of empathy?"

He grins, "Yes, Marty, that still sounds good – but, in addition, the next house that gets bought will be bigger than what I have now – and this time, I get to slap the bucks down!"

I say nothing, just turn, open the door and leave.

A startled Indian woman in the hallway ducks back into her room. It looks like the Group Areas are starting to fray around the edges in these liminal, marginalized spaces.

Joubert and the bored Security Guard don't even throw me a glance as I stride through the lobby, looking like an ogre... No doubt they've seen far worse.

I scan the dimly lit parking lot before scurrying across to my car, bag bouncing on my back despite my taut jacket, an edge of the EE machine digging into the space between my shoulder blades.

Bag locked in the boot I sit at the wheel of my car, waiting for Dan to emerge. His little VW is parked quietly off to one side, next to a BMW to minimize its chances of being stolen.

He doesn't come.

I see a woman in short coat and high heels clop her way through the gate, heading for the motel. She looks hurried and furtive, but is obviously proud of her smooth, pale, long legs. She may be on her way to Room 129.

Two meetings for the price of one, perhaps, Dan? If so, he's still careful to be staying on the right side of the Immorality Act.

I start the car, wondering at how familiar people can suddenly become complete strangers.

Chapter 7
Sibusiso at Hope's Folly

I follow Nombuso into the hallway, swinging my gaze across wide sagging ceilings, green grunge hiding in the dark corners underneath bobbing spider-webs. The hall is wide and airy and flows through into a massive space, cluttered with a naked, lumpy green couch, a few hard chairs and a TV. Rooms with closed doors are sealed off from the corridor and it feels like I am propelled after Nombuso, through the gaping lounge and wide-open front doors onto the *stoep*. This is one massive *stoep*; its red concrete is warm from sun leaking through the dense crimson bougainvillea hanging from a sturdy wooden frame overhead.

There are steps leading down from the *stoep* towards fields of cows, circled by the tick-tick-ticking of an electric fence cord. The steps have wide sloping concrete banisters; both the left and right side are occupied by a person lying on them, feet facing downwards, on long green cushions no doubt stolen from the couch. There's a short bearded man on the right banister and a large plump white woman on the left.

Nombuso is slapping palms with the man and I notice the woman is asleep, vest and short denim skirt revealing large rolls of pinky-brown flesh.

"Hey Sibusiso, meet Thulani."

The man swings his legs off the banister and sits at an awkward angle, smiling stiffly up at me. He has no shirt on and his short trunk is powerfully muscled with tight and disciplined curls of chest hair.

He raises a hand, but does not offer it – I guess slaps have to be earned.

The woman stirs and holds her arms out, feeling the base of the banister and adjusting her position, so as not to fall off. It looks like a skill that has taken many sun cycles to master.

"Eh –?" She grunts and I see her eyes are open. She is watching me as I stand self-consciously at the top of the stairs.

Nombuso barks a short laugh: "Jill, meet Sibusiso, I have just fetched him from Fort Napier."

Jill's eyes flare and she struggles to sit up, losing her balance. Nombuso steps forward and catches a hand, stopping her rolling backwards off the banister.

"Why have you brought him here, Nombuso?" Thulani sounds blunt and looks sour.

Jill has regained her balance and slides off the step, skirt hitching up around her hips and I glance away politely. Inside, I am angry, unsure now why she has indeed brought me here. Am I the local mad entertainment?

Nombuso perches next to Thulani and gestures at me to sit opposite, where Jill has perched, skirt rearranged modestly.

I lean, standing, ready to move quickly should I need to.

"Sibusiso was in the college march. His friend was killed next to him. He is finding that hard to deal with – as would any of us."

I am not happy to hear my experiences being spilled so easily in front of people I do not know. I turn to stare angrily as the cows move slowly across the field, calling to each other, eating grass. I have no way back, unless I walk to the top road and catch a lift from a taxi.

Nombuso must have stood up. I feel her warmth behind me on the step, she is touching my shoulder: "I thought you could join us Sibusiso, we all work for change here, for a place where no one gets shot and all are free to live and move in peace, wherever they are – you know, Freedom Charter and all."

I wipe a fly from my face and watch how slowly the cows move in the deep heat. The smell of their waste is strong, the flies many. Inside me, the Beast stirs.

"Why have you not asked us first, Nombuso?" Thulani's deep voice rumbles through my head.

"I only thought of it recently," she says. "We have lost one member and I know Sibusiso feels as we do."

How lost? Is it like one loses a pen or a penny? Am I a thing or a man?

I turn on the steps, looking up the slope at them, wiping sticky sweat from my forehead with the back of my hand. "And if I chose not to join?"

"Feel free to go, brother," Thulani is standing now, as if enjoying being taller than me on the sloping stairs. He folds his arms to square his chest and shoulders.

The Beast inside growls and – I do not know why – it makes me laugh. It is a short burst of laughter and then I think; why do we square our bodies against each other, when the *boere* shoot us from a safe distance?

I shake my head: "No, my brother, indeed I think I will join you."

Nombuso smiles: "Good, should I show you your room?"

I must have looked blank, because after a pause, she says: "We have a vacated room you can spend the night in – you are on weekend leave after all." She's watching my face carefully.

Tchhhaagghh! Thulani spits against a nearby hanging bougainvillea flower: "How do we know he is not a spy?"

"Hacker has done his homework," Nombuso says shortly.

It takes me a moment to realise she is talking about someone else – someone who has seemingly accessed my computer files and records.

"You have hacked my college computer?"

She shrugs, a little embarrassed - but just a little bit, it seems. "We needed to be sure before we asked you, 'Biso."

"And this is how you ask me?"

"It is not safe just to ask, you know how brother fights against brother and how the *boere* buy our souls."

I feel ill in the heat. I turn to step down onto the strip of grassy verge that runs in a riot of weeds and tussocks before the cattle fence.

The fence tick-tick-ticks in my face and I place a hand on it, arm jerking with the jolt of current. There is a suppressed scream behind me, but I ignore it, locking my right hand hard on the black wire, gritting my teeth against the numbness spreading up my arm.

My life has been hacked.

It's not the files I mind, but the voice records of my life, started as I left home for the first time, these recordings I make now on that tiny disc my father gave me, small yes, but costing many *rands* I have no doubt. Precious are my thoughts; precious are these words that fuel me – so precious, that I placed another password on them.

A name no one could guess... (*Busisiwe.*)

I release my fist and turn, flexing my tingling hand, finding it hard to feel my fingers. All three of them just stand and watch me, as if dumb statues.

"How much did Hacker hack?" I ask.

"Just enough to know where your sympathies lie; your word files and e-mails."

Relief washes over me, not my secured voice files then. I do not feel quite so... violated. So, they sought to know too who is master of *my* politics. It is indeed not something open to straight questions. Still, I continue to feel dirtied, resentful.

"Take me back to hospital," I say, "the mad folk are more honest."

It is not Nombuso who comes down off the stairs, but Thulani. "Sorry, brother, I have indeed been rude. I wish now you would stay."

I look at him – he too, locks my gaze.

He is some ten years or more older than me and I see something of Father's forthrightness in his eyes.

I hold out my numbed hand. He grins and slaps it into life.

"Welcome home, son," Father waves me in to our house, a small brick hut on the bottom of *Baas* Esterhuyze's farm. The house is changed and none of my sisters, nor my brother, are there to greet me.

I am disappointed, confused, but still happy to see my father. Are they at school then? But it is night outside as he closes the front door and leads me to the back.

"I have something for you, my son," he says, opening the back door.

A black, snarling beast bounds in and there is only time to gurgle, as its huge jaws clamp my throat.

Uggghh! uggghhh! ugghhh!

I am in a strange bed, coughing my throat out, my eyes dripping from shock.

Is this another dream layer, a dream within a dream within a...? The thin blue curtains in the square-boxed window glow with early sun's light.

I sit up and swivel in my bed – it is a simple room, an open wardrobe which hangs empty, a bookshelf with one book lying flat – an old yellow-paged collection of stories by Can Themba, banned for many decades now.

The book anchors my memories, pulling me into the nowness of my body. Yes, I read 'The Suit' last night; as for me, I have no suit. This is no dream, I cough, my throat sore.

There is damp in the room, the ceiling spattered with dark green and black patches. I feel cold despite the sun leaking in through wispy curtains and pull on red T-shirt and brown corduroy trousers.

I do not feel well, but there is no father here and my mother is long gone, a fading memory of warm skin, food, smiles and the occasional sting of a slap.

I need to move, before my eyes start to drip again, before the Beast grabs my throat. Is it that I must every day re-chain this Beast prowling inside me, gnawing at my insides in its rage and frustration?

Get moving, Sib – the door is part open, the door-handle long gone. I cough and push it with my left hand, lurching into the wide-open expanse of what Nombuso has called 'the lounge'.

The room is empty, but I feel the call of the sun through the open back door. Stepping outside I wrap my arms tighter around my body to stem the coughs, for Thulani and Nombuso are sitting on the balustrades of the sloping steps, talking to each other in low voices.

They stop and look at me as I approach the steps and I wonder what or whom they were talking about.

Nombuso stands up with a concerned frown on her face.

"Are you alright 'Sibo, you look ill?"

"A cough, a small thing," I say, uncomfortable with her concern. "Thank you for the room. Is it time to go back to the hospital?"

"*Hayi*, no..." She laughs. "Surely you do not like the place that much? You are only due back from weekend leave at nine tonight. I thought I would take you into *Imbali* to meet Mamma Makosi, someone who will offer you a safe space should anything happen here."

I cough: "What do you mean?"

She shrugs her shoulders: "The police have eyes everywhere – we keep quiet about what we do, but no place is safe. Mamma Makosi though –" she smiles and the sun warms my body even more "– has been safe for many years now. It will be hard for anyone to find their way around her!"

Thulani stands up and nods at me. From behind me, I smell cooking eggs and bacon drifting on the cool breeze filtering through the house.

My stomach burbles in excitement and Thulani laughs: "Come, Brother, time to eat first."

It is Jill who cooks and a fine meal it is, although the bacon cuts my throat and I need to drink much water to soothe it.

I thank Jill, Nombuso picks up the bike helmet and we walk outside to where her faithful bike stands waiting. I hear the birds calling, spotting the cheerful flash of a crested barbet winging up into the blue-gum canopy above us. (Although my father has no degrees, he understands many things, teaching me much about our fellow animals.)

I cough as the helmet closes over my head, bumping against my shoulders and then we are off in a bouncing snarl of the bike's engine. Nombuso stands up slightly to avoid the worst of the bounces, but I am too scared, groaning as my privates take a further bruising.

We sweep past the quarry and the lake now on our right and I sigh and cough with relief as we swerve onto smooth road, Nombuso settling back to gun her engine with aggression.

I don't mind, as I need to clutch her warm body tightly, hands wrapped around her stomach, the occasional tantalizing bounce of a breast brushing the tops of my arms and hands through her clothes.

I lose track of the journey as we weave and sway across roads, but at one point we slow down and I hear her shouted curses: "Fucking *boere*... route."

She swings violently to the left, the road surface jarring again, the houses increasingly smaller, more dilapidated and dotted with shacks and broken clearance ruins.

We grind to a halt next to a row of small houses hidden amongst a swelling swathe of shacks and *spaza* shops.

Nombuso kicks her bike stand down and I swing my numbed right leg off with some difficulty.

In contrast to that growing sea of shacks, the house we are parked outside is small, brown-bricked and solid, raised slightly on a few steps. A man steps through the door and down the steps, approaching us with easy and confident assurance. He is big and bald with variously numbered tattoos that remind me of stories about the Prison Gangs in Cape Town, although his skin is as dark as anyone's.

He throws me an evil-looking glance that starts my cough again, but Nombuso nods and touches my shoulder and the man relaxes, just a little.

"Come in then, Mamma is expecting you." His voice is more high-pitched than I expected.

Nombuso stops him with a raised right hand and then indicates towards me with her left: "Numbers, meet Sibusiso, Sib – this is Numbers."

He gives me a tight smile, like a snake. At least I won't have to ask him where he got his name from.

He stands aside to wave us in and I see a *panga* glinting behind the swirl of his long coat.

Inside, the house has a small entrance room, with a couch and chair, rooms leading off right, left and behind. Given the size of the exterior, that must be all.

Nombuso sits down on the couch and waves at me to join her. Numbers stands by the door like a bodyguard.

The couch is a soft balm to my aching privates and I sink into it with relief.

The door dead opposite opens and a large woman with a white blouse and knee length black skirt steps in, moving surprisingly lightly in her squared and sensible black shoes. She gives us a slight bow and her beaded and braided locks splay across her shoulders. We spring to our feet, almost wrenched up, by the magnetism of her beaming face.

"Mamma!" Nombuso looks down in respect: "I have brought a new recruit, in case he should need some safe time within your house. He is –"

"Welcome, Sibusiso Mchunu!"

I start, and I can see even Nombuso looks unsettled.

"I trust you are starting to feel better from your ailment? Still, you will need to go back to the healing house tonight."

The 'healing house' – does she mean Fort Napier?

"Come, sit," she says, "and don't look so worried, for I know many people, including those within the hospital."

Ahhhh, I think, Jabu?

She drops her bulk onto the chair and folds her arms in front of her. We sit again, but she is now looking above my left shoulder.

It makes my hair prickle. I glance to my left, but see nothing except Numbers cleaning his fingernails with a small knife.

I look at her again. Her broad smile has slipped into a slight one, with a slightly sad looking quirk to her lips on the left side of her face.

"You carry *amadlozi* with you, my son."

I wonder which of my ancestors she has seen, but she does not wait for me to ask: "And you look ill – never mind, I have just the right thing for you."

With a roll of her broad hips she is up again and into the room on the right; I catch a flash of hanging flasks and bottles; a room that looks as busy as a pharmacy. She closes the door and I look at Nombuso.

"Mamma's a *sangoma*," she says, "and a very good one too!"

She returns with a small bottle of blackish liquid, which is so sour and sharp on the throat it just makes me cough even more. I do not wish to know what is in there, but all she does is chuckle. "Nasty things often bring the body into better spaces," she says, "as long as you become aware of whom else you may be carrying."

"Who, Mamma?"

She shrugs: "I don't know, but nor is it for me to say; it's for you to find out, my boy."

There's beeping noise from near the door and Numbers makes a sign with his hand.

Mamma nods. "I'm sorry – it's always good to see you, Nombuso, but as you know I am busy – I have more waiting to see me."

"Sure, Mamma," Nombuso stands to take her leave.

A small boy walks in through the door behind; "Mamma?" She holds her arms out to him, hoists him up and turns to me. "His parents are beyond our borders."

I notice she speaks as if we own the borders and spaces within.

"You're a smart boy, you'll remember this address should you need it, I'm sure. I can't give you the address I'm afraid," she says. "Too many bad people want it."

I step forward and nod respectfully. "Never mind, Mamma, I will remember." She smiles.

Somehow, I know I will be back.

"If you need a bit of money my boy, just ask Numbers – he is multi-skilled and is our accountant too."

I smile in return, but with grateful surprise; Numbers just opens the door without a word.

The old English cliché comes to mind: 'never judge a book by its cover.'

Many 'books' surround me now – and I need to be able to read well indeed, if I am to survive.

Nombuso hands me a helmet and Numbers ushers an old woman into the house, frail and bent.

I put the helmet on, without a cough.

The *stoep* is warm again. The cattle continue to graze in the fields below. I sit on a sloping cushion along a concrete arm of the downward steps, hearing the occasional lowing. The smell of cow dung swirls in on the hot breeze sweeping up the valley. The town below, Pietermaritzburg, uMgungundlovu, is smeared in smog, gasping smoke at the base of these hills. I lie back and doze, the house behind me breathing in time to the gusts of winds wafting through the front door, 'whooshing' out through the back – soothing sounds, with little inside the house to disturb.

Lightning sheets flare like lamps on the inside of my eyelids and I startle awake, mouth drooling, neck stiff and sore. The town has vanished in a swathe of black clouds, pulsing with flashes of light, staccato sounds grumbling up the valley towards me.

I rush inside the large lounge with the cushion, wet wind chasing me, managing to heave the door partly closed behind me. Thulani and Jill are there already holding buckets; they hand one to me.

"Check the rooms on your side of the house;" says Thulani,

"We are never sure where leaks will appear – each storm leaks though in different places."

"It's just us," says Jill. "Nombuso has gone to fill her bike for your trip back to the hospital."

The farmhouse dribbles and rattles with a sudden burst of heavy rain and hailstones on the corrugated roof. I check the laundry and a small room off the hallway to the right, reeking with stale cats' piss. No leak though - the hallway itself is surprisingly dry, as is the kitchen beyond. My room though, last on the left when I return to the lounge, is pouring like Victoria Falls.

I place the bucket, wondering how quickly it will fill, shivering in the empty room. My bed still smells faintly of night terrors and a lonely illness.

There is a rattling clunk next door and I push my door open again to look out. Jill has hooked up a heater near the couch lounge and is knocking it with a spanner, seemingly to get it working.

Stomach softening smells come from the kitchen – it must be Thulani cooking, Nombuso is not yet back. Jill gestures at me to come in and she sidles onto the couch.

Instead, I go and stand under the bougainvillea, so thick as to reduce this torrent of rain to just a few spurting trickles in places. A dribble wets the back of my neck, but I peer down the darkening hill.

Above me, I hear a clucking noise – chickens? Chickens cannot fly. I peer up into the tangled maze of branches over my head. There. A cat. No, it is no ordinary cat – it is small, but spotted, with a striped tail. A civet. I have seen pictures of them at school, but this one is trembling above my head – and I am no longer so alone. It flashes its paws and is gone.

I peer down the hill again.

A ghostly bird with a large beak like a blade flashes past me.

I shiver. It is a bird that is more than a bird, I suspect, although what it is called, I do not know.

There. An erratic light is lurching up the hill, but I hear nothing except the rattle of rain. The light itself is blurred, muted, fighting against the dark, but grows steadily stronger and brighter until I hear the background whine of a struggling engine.

The bike roars past in a spray of wet mud and I retreat back into the house. Thulani is standing next to the heater, a grilled chicken, *samp* and beans wait on the small table.

Jill comes in with a tray piled with plates and cheap glasses filled with peach cordial.

I walk past into the hallway and Nombuso comes stamping in.

She grins at me and places her helmet on a small chair near the back door. "Smells like I'm just in time for supper – yum, yum!"

It is indeed yum, yum! Afterwards, Thulani brings in a tray of baked biscuits and Jill brings out a bottle of whisky from her and Thulani's room.

I manage just a short, sharp sip of the whisky and gag – sticking after that to the sweet peach drink. The biscuits are nice, however, even though they look a shade green.

The conversation drifts to my stay in the hospital – they are curious no doubt, and I tell them stories of electric torture and medication *sjamboks*. I have seen little of this myself, but then I have not been to the wards at the back of the hospital. Yet.

They grow quiet when I mention Dr. Van Deventer and the Box, though – Nombuso gives me a strange look, asking me to confirm the Box does indeed work.

"Yes," I say, "Not perfectly, it's a bit blurred and vague, almost like background noise with jerky faded video images, but I gather from the doctor's response, it was real enough."

Nombuso looks at Jill, who nods slowly. "Checks out with some intel I've heard recently," Jill says.

I have no idea how she knows these things. Perhaps voices have spoken with her; spirit voices escaping from the Box.

As for me, their voices fade and return too, as if someone is playing with volume control. Only Nkulunkulu, God Himself, is capable of doing that, so it must be that He has come to Earth now to share my fate. Inside me, I feel the purring of a great Beast in my stomach, making me smile with pleasure.

Thulani is saying how the Box might be a weapon, a communications bomb that could blast through the apartheid wall. I struggle to make sense of his words, because I have no sense of bombs brewing in my head, nor walls, just the peace of God that is spreading through this room and time itself is slowing.

Nombuso looks at me. "So," she asks, "will you steal the Box for us?"

I laugh and laugh. She shakes her head, but it looks as if it is moving in slow motion. She is leaning forward to look into my eyes and I see her bosom stretch against her white T-shirt.

"I'm taking you back to the hospital, but please keep quiet when I sign you back in, Sibusiso – and just go straight to bed. I will pack some sandwiches and chicken in your bag, should you get hungry during the night."

"Sure," I say, "for God can live through chickens too."

"Please, Sibusiso, whatever you do, don't say anything – just keep quiet, all right?"

I nod, wondering why my head and tongue feel clumsy, but perhaps all becomes clumsy, in the presence of God.

I find myself outside, unsure of how I got there. Nombuso places the helmet over my head. I feel some dampness on my face and my bag is heavy on my back.

"Whatever you do, don't let go, okay?"

"Surely," I say.

"And what did we ask you to do?"

"Steal the doctor's Box," I say.

The words and the wetness wake me from this strange and slow state of bliss.

Nombuso taps my bag. "No more biscuits in here, okay Sib? And please, for God's sake, hang onto me!"

It is for more than the sake of God that I hang onto Nombuso for the long, slow, beautiful ride back to the lunatic asylum.

Chapter 8
Martin's Relationships

The phone rings and I assume it is Dan, so I dawdle out of the kitchen where I've just fed Jacky. It's a Saturday, so I'm up later than usual, just after eight.

Still, it's an early call for the weekend, so I let the phone ring until the auto-message kicks in; perfunctory, almost abrupt - and certainly meant to discourage.

"Van Deventer here, please leave a message."

"Hello –?" The voice is feminine, hesitant and unsure of itself: "Marlene here, I was at the PsycSoc protest meeting and you gave me your card. I – uh –"

I snatch the phone out of its base.

"Hello, hello, Martin here."

There is silence. My voice cutting across the auto-message seems to have stunted the flow of her words even more.

"Hello, um Marlene, are you there?"

"Uh, hello, Doctor..."

"Call me Martin," I say, "Just Martin."

"Hello, err, Martin, thank you for giving me card. I'm hoping it means that you uhm, maybe want to meet up – and not that you think I'm mad?"

I chuckle: "Ja, of course! That's once we've bumped into each other, sort of, I just thought it might be nice to be in charge the next time, if that's alright with you I mean..." Shit – I'm a man who's still *kak* with words for women.

She giggles softly: "Maybe, depends what you mean by 'in charge', of course..."

Warmth stings my face: "Just that I'd like to meet on purpose, nothing more, and only if both parties are agreeable."

She chuckles, louder this time: "Are you a lawyer as well, Martin? I was just thinking you meant a coffee or something like that, but perhaps I'm wrong?"

"Perfect." I lean against the hallway wall, wilfully stopping the flow of stupid words. Jacky comes in from the kitchen to lick my toes. I have only a short towel dressing gown on.

"So when do you want to meet up?" She asks.

I wince. Jacky has moved up to lick the healing scab on my right heel.

"Is late morning – about eleven – too soon?" There is a brief silence and I push Jacky away with my left foot, cursing myself, wondering if I sound too desperate, too needy.

"Sure," she says, "I can't stay too long, though, about an hour or so, so where do you want to meet up?"

"How about here?" I ask impulsively and then curse myself again; stupid, stupid, van Deventer, much too *voorbarig*.

There's an even longer silence and I rack my brains for a diplomatic way to retrieve my words, to rescue the conversation.

"Okay," she says, 'I see your home address is on here, presumably it's your private practice?"

"Yes," I say, unable to say anything more.

"Eleven o'clock fine?" she asks.

"Yes," I manage, although my voice sounds squeaky, even shrill to my ears.

"See you then, Martin."

She hangs up and I put the phone down, wondering why - despite my ease with therapeutic conversations - personal conversations have become increasingly difficult.

I push Jacky away from my heel again, suddenly aware of the impact of Marlene's soft, feminine tones, as well as her agreement to come here.

I have an erection pushing uncomfortably against the folds of my dressing gown.

Talk about *voorbarig*.

I'm alerted by Jacky's barking and glance up at the clock; it's five minutes to eleven. I've barely made it back from Choose 'N Cash with a stale pecan pie, clumsily arranged on a flat white plate. I leave it in the kitchen and stroll through with stiff nonchalance; Jacky is snuffling at the front door and wagging her long tail.

I open the door and Marlene stands there with her hands coyly laced in front of her, tight jeaned and with a floaty sky blue blouse teasing at her slight figure underneath. The slight breeze fans across us.

Jesus, it's been a long time.

I invite her in, my left hand crooked low in front of me to hide the bulge in my trousers, which feels like Mount Fucking Everest.

Marlene stoops and pats Jacky, seemingly at ease with animals. I guide her down to the lounge: "Tea or coffee?"

"Six Roses please, if you have it, Martin."

I escape to the kitchen and re-boil the kettle for the fourth time, which simultaneously allows my erection to deflate. I gather two mugs of tea, plates, a knife and the sticky pecan pie onto a tray and saunter through.

Marlene is leafing through my coffee table paperback, a soiled and banned copy of Fanon's *Wretched of the Earth*, seemingly tossed nonchalantly alongside Tidhar's *Osama*. I hope it'll impress, although I also hope she doesn't ask me much about it, as I've failed to get past page thirty of the Fanon.

She doesn't say anything, though, just closes the book hurriedly and twists round in her seat to face me. I see her eyes are half-closed, her mouth half-open. I place the tray down, sit next to her and in one easy, soundless movement she presses up against me, wraps her arms tightly around my waist, her face close, almost level with mine. I feel her nipples and firm breasts pressing against my chest - she is not wearing a bra — and the pressure within my trousers surges again.

I groan and quiver as she kisses me. She must have seen my erection and decided there was no need for pecan pie.

I step backwards towards the bedroom, not wanting to do anything with Jacky around. The dog is already growling with sudden jealous dislike, but I push her away as Marlene and I stagger into the bedroom. I manage to swing the door shut on my dog with a shaking left hand; as it slams shut with a resounding bang I hear a startled yelp.

I turn to find Marlene teetering on one leg, dragging her jeans awkwardly off with one hand. Not the easiest of clothes to escape from; she couldn't have anticipated this.

Neither had I, but with eternal optimism I had chosen trousers with loose ties to maximize speed of removal, just in case. I have them and my *scants* off just as Marlene finishes removing her jeans and frilly black thong.

I enter her from behind in a desperately eager rush, almost blind with pleasure; she braces herself against the bed with her hands.

Through the haze of pleasure, I notice dimly that I have not removed or turned around the picture of Suzette at the Umgeni Bridge from the bedside cabinet.

Shit... Marlene is soft and moist inside; ohh, Goddd, who caressss!

I ejaculate with a burst of pleasure – and with the faintest of feelings that something is not quite right.

Sibusiso is different.

I sense it as I look at the young man on the other side of the desk, eyeing me carefully behind his slightly lowered head and eyelids. His hair is a little thicker, his body a little straighter in the chair than this time last week.

Still, the wound on his head gapes at me – this time a little more openly, a little more *rawly* – although on the surface it looks more blunted, more healed. Inside me, though, I have no direct sense of that.

He lifts his head and raises his right eyebrow at me: "Something wrong, Doctor?"

That's it; he takes more control of the space, as if a little more assured of himself here.

"Not at all, Sibusiso," I lean forward, pleased, placing my open hands on the desk space between us. "You seem a little more animated today."

He looks at me blankly.

"...a little more active," I supply, knowing he would have gobbled the corresponding Zulu word, should I have been clever enough to have supplied it. As it is, I am still suffused with residual pride at having told him to '*hlala phansi*.'

"I feel my spirit returning to me," he says, and a slow smile breaks his face open.

I am pleased; progress indeed. "What's made the difference, do you think, Sibusiso?"

He shrugs: "Perhaps the pills, perhaps the words with Jabu, or new friends beyond these walls, perhaps all this and more."

I notice he does not mention us.

"Tell me more," I am leaning forward now, silently egging his spirit up into his face and mouth.

But this seems to disturb him. He sits back and his smile is only a faint whisper on his face; instead, his eyes have clouded over. "I see more to life now than Mandla's death," he says, shortly. He stretches back in his chair and swings his gaze slowly around the room.

I mirror him just a bit, easing off my intensity by withdrawing my hands from the table, which were perhaps too eager, too grasping? Go slowly, Van Deventer, the man is recovering from PTSD and a severe depression, so coax gently, don't wheedle.

He is standing, moving around the room, looking at other pictures on the wall. I wonder what he makes of these neutral photos, pictures of sea, of mountains, of forests, with nothing human or controversial in them. Perhaps I should treat them as informal Rorschach blots and see what meanings he projects onto them.

"What do you see in that picture, Sibusiso?" I nail him with that question to the picture of Cathedral Peak spreading in front of him, from the Drakensberg Mountains, not too many miles from here.

He turns to glance at me: "The *Ukhahlamba* Mountains, it is not far from my father's home and his father before him and his father..." He turns to face me fully. "Until long before the white man came."

His psyche has become colonized with identity politics that split us again, raising space the size of a mountain between us. I stand and move around the desk to ensure there are no other physical barriers between us.

He folds his arm across his chest and stands firm.

I hesitate and stop, a few paces off. "You miss your father, then."

The political is ever personal. His eyes mist over and he turns his back on me, afraid again to share his vulnerability and pain.

I know now what he responds to. Some psychologists aspire to the blank slates of analysts, looking for the projections of patients, revealing little. Sibusiso will give little, unless he receives. And he is smart enough to know what is real, what is not. I am realizing there is not even a hint of psychosis in his presentation – if anything, he sees the world *too* clearly.

"I miss my father too," I offer, knowing leaking personal details is an anathema to many psychologists, but I sense Sibusiso will only respond to the real details in any relationship. I feel strangely relieved, offering up such a raw and truthful sentence, for there is a part of me that feels like a prostitute, providing 'relationships' for money. I want to be more than a psychic receptacle.

He turns around to look at me. "Where is he, Doctor?"

"Martin," I say, wishing to retrieve lost territory quickly and to push on, as if – colonizing?

"Where is he... Doctor?"

He will not yield ground easily.

"He lives in Durban."

His face frowns: "A car's drive away for you, surely?"

"Sometimes there is more than space that separates us, Sibusiso."

His arms unfold and his restless hands find room in the pockets of his loose orange institutional trousers. I am too sophisticated to interpret this as evasiveness, as the body language people would have us believe. Instead, I am sure he is just unsure what to do with his hands. I am aware my own hands are clasped in front of me.

But he is smiling again: "Indeed... Martin, we are now close physically, but still you know little of the details of my world."

"Then tell me," I say.

His eyelids narrow momentarily. "Wouldn't you rather see, with your own mind?"

I am confused, for just a moment, until I remember my – that is – *our* EE machine, with a brief surge of excitement.

"You want to try the Box again – and are willing for me to read *you* this time?"

He pulls a hand out of his pocket, splaying the five fingers on his right palm in front of his chest. "Five seconds Doctor, that's all you'll get. Perhaps more next time, if you make good use of those seconds."

It is better than nothing. An ideal opportunity to test whether our Box has been properly fixed, to test whether 'local is *lekker*' and good enough. This time though, I will lock the door.

Sibusiso has brushed past me and sat down again. I catch the faint whiff of a body deodorant, faintly feminine to my nose.

I turn and rummage for the key in the top left drawer and then click open the latch lock holding the test cupboard secure. I bend down to the bottom shelf, flicking some MMPI forms off the Box pushed out of sight against the far right hand corner. My house is not safe, the hospital has guards – and no one will suspect I brazenly keep the replacement locked and hidden here.

I swing it round with pride and place it delicately onto the desk.

Sibusiso's eyes widen, "It's different!"

"I broke it by accident, but we managed to fix it. I'm sorry, but that is why I cancelled our last appointment."

He eyes me, but I am too afraid to tell him what really happened. I have no doubt he will clam up if he knew the SB were after the Box too. I keep my face open and candid.

Psychologists can make bloody good liars.

His gaze flickers down to the Box and I secure the headgear.

He looks across to me as I sit, head caps in place. He holds his splayed right hand up again: "Five seconds, Doctor!"

I nod and pull the lever.

I am struggling, fighting hard, body and breath wrapped tight by people hauling me out of the back of a van. I catch a glimpse of an aging black man, face crumpled with emotional pain, standing behind the people pulling at me, his hands wringing in distress. Still, I feel betrayal biting through my body.

I blink and notice Sibusiso has removed his head cap.

"What did you see, Doctor?"

"Your father," I say.

He nods – and this time, he cries openly.

And so it is; that we talk about fathers.

It is late at night by the time I pluck up the courage to call my own father. The phone rings three times and I hover the receiver close to its base, almost hanging up.

Almost – but not quite.

Always encouraging others, it is time to practice what I preach.

"*Ja, di's Hettie van Deventer hier.*"

"Ma?"

"Martin..."

I haven't called in three years. She seems at a loss for further words, but has said my name with such feeling; I feel a wave of guilt wash over me.

Still, it's not all my fault.

"How you doing, Ma?"

"Martin..." she says again. For a moment I think Jacky is whimpering at my feet and glance down, but then remember she's in the lounge with Marlene.

It must be my mother. "Hi, Ma," I say again.

"Why are you only phoning us now?" Her Afrikaans is terse; it's as if she has cloaked her tears in an angry and brusque question. I admit to myself it is a fair question too.

"*Jammer*, Ma, but I wasn't sure what to say to Pa after our last fight."

"Three years Martin, three years..."

We're a proud and stubborn family indeed.

I shift uncomfortably on the hallway stool, wondering what to say next. I had thought of role-playing in advance or scripting a few questions, but that seemed too staged, too false.

Marlene pads into the hallway, demurely dressed in a yellow towelling robe, and she gives me a 'thumbs up'. Renewed vigour flushes through me and I decide to just open my mouth and trust it. The start, after all, is often the hardest part.

"I'd like to come down for the weekend, Ma, to try and put things right with Pa. I miss you and – er, him too. I want to put things right again. If I can."

There is silence on the other end. Dead silence. I realise the 'secrecy' button has been pushed on the other side. Marlene raises her eyebrows at me and I shrug.

Click. "Martin?"

"*Ja*, Ma?"

"Your father says okay, as long as there's no political talk, alright?"

"Okay, Ma," I smile, but tightly, with apprehension as well as relief.

"We've got some shopping to do, but we can see you after eleven on Saturday. You can stay in the spare room overnight if you want."

"Thanks, Ma." I won't pack an overnight bag though. A

weekend is too long after three years of silence. Baby steps.

"All right, good night, Martin." She hangs up, sounding suddenly and strangely tired – but then, it is late, even if they are retired.

I stand up and slowly place the phone in the cradle. Marlene is standing behind me, arms around me, holding me close. Her damp hair smells slightly of tea tree oil shampoo and I feel her soft breasts against my shoulder blades, through my thin cotton shirt. I move her hands down to my bulging crotch.

We make the bed somehow and undress feverishly.

I'm still too desperate, too urgent, too excited, coming quickly and before her. She writhes and groans a split second after me, but the split second is a second too late.

I lie spent, holding her, wondering whether she is protecting my ego.

Then I see the photo of Suzette again. Shit, I'd still forgotten – to hide that, or to put it away. Marlene seems to be dozing in my arms, but I am suddenly wide-awake.

Marlene looks so like Suzette, just with shorter hair. So uncannily like her...

Her eyes open and she looks up at me: "What's wrong, darling?"

I look at her and feel myself tensing even further. Somehow, I *know*. In fact, I think I'd always known, but didn't want to think it.

She'd told me she'd been expelled from her family as a rebel – the *'swart skaap'* – a black sheep story that – with hindsight – resonated too closely to my own. I would have realised earlier – if only it hadn't been for the shape of her breasts beneath her blouse.

I roll away from her and sit up. "Who are you? Really?"

Her eyelids flutter and she rolls over the other way and feels under the bed. I panic and hold a pillow up in front of me, but all she sits up with is a cigarette and a lighter.

I put the pillow down as she lights up. I am too frightened

to tell her not to. Marlene had always told me she was a fervent anti-smoker, just like me.

"So," she says, blowing a smoke ring at me: "Some real pleasure at last! Have you tried rebuilding your Thought Machine again, Doctor?"

Chapter 9
Sibusiso's Flight from Folly

Real silence is rare in a psychiatric institute, the lunatic asylum. I lie awake for the perfect moment, but none arrives. Always someone talks, grunts or wheezes, even in the deepest dark of night.

So the nights and days peel across the week and I have my therapy again on Thursday – we talk about the pain of fathers, even though neither of us is, as yet, a father. The doctor admits he struggles with his father too and I wonder how best to make things right with my own father. I test my doctor, and get him to bring out his Magic Thought Box. So it is that I guiltily note the details of where Dr. van Deventer hides it – and the key with which he accesses it.

I sent him my thoughts and the image of betrayal in five sharp seconds and he says at the end that he will organize a 'family' session soon – but, much though I want to, I don't think that I can wait for such a session. I don't know how long before the doctor moves his Box: or indeed someone else – like that dry and dangerous Dr. James – perhaps finds and confiscates it.

I lie in bed, my stomach is full from the evening curry I both chose and insisted upon. I smile contentedly, remembering the woman's angry and resistant face, but she'd eventually given in, as the line of people waiting for food mounted behind me. I'd stood with firm panther feet, until she'd slapped the curry messily onto my plate.

I think of Nombuso and her promises. I need to get the Box to her and we will have a weapon against the *boere*. I was not thinking straight then – but now I wonder how exactly they hope to wield this 'weapon'.

Guilt too, I feel, looking for any excuse again tonight not to move – Dumisani there in the opposite bunk is talking to God;

the night staff are restless and pace the dorm every hour.

For I find, despite myself, I do like the doctor – and I have no real wish to steal from him.

I lie quietly, unmoving, and start to tremble as the gas gathers around me. I know what is coming next and there is nothing I can do to stop it. There are loud shots and I fall forward to catch Mandla, but it is too late, his right eye weeps blood and his brains leak onto my trousers. I scream, but wake, mouth choked, my scream just part of a strangled and recurring nightmare. I open my mouth and gasp. Really, I have no voice.

I do not want to lose any more friends.

I cannot wait any longer. There is no perfect moment, no complete stillness.

I roll off my bunk and swing my rucksack from beneath my bed, while Dumisani continues to praise God. I hoist my bag onto my back and tie my *takkies*. I freeze as a staff nurse drifts by, but he is heading to the TV in the lounge, unconcerned by we who should be sleeping.

I pad warily past the nurses' station and peer into the lounge. Both men are lost in a rerun of the Premiership game between Sundowns and Chiefs. One chews on a piece of dried sausage, it looks like Zandile. I wait for something to happen; their attention seems wavering, uncommitted.

A man falls in the penalty area. "Penalty!" shouts the nurse I do not recognise, standing up. Zandile barks his disagreement, enabling me to walk with quiet steps behind them and through into the wider hospital corridor beyond.

I turn right with no hesitation, walking with sureness in order to allay any suspicions.

Right, left, right again – ah, there is the doctor's room. I am glad this is not a secure or forensic setting; the place is indeed quiet at this time, although the floor whispers beneath my feet.

I push against the door, relieved that it opens. The cleaners often forget to re-lock doors and security do not come here – for who would break *into* a madhouse?

Only madmen like me, surely. I hope this Box is worth any trouble it may bring.

I flick the light switch and close the door, but know I don't have long as the light through the door-pane is a dead giveaway to anyone passing, the doctor's work ethic not noted for midnight office appearances, I am sure.

I step across to his desk and pull at the left sided drawer. It does not give and I curse. No doubt he locked the drawer and took the key with him. He guards the Box with the utmost caution; I have seen this in the reverence with which he treats it.

I have no time for niceties. I wedge a chisel stolen from our occupational therapy workspace into the small gap between key-lock and desk. I have no hammer, so step back and kick the wedged chisel. It splinters the wood and lock with a brief but loud bang.

My hand shakes as I find the cupboard key under a pile of papers. I drop the key and it spins towards the test-cupboard. For one heart-stopping moment I think it will disappear under the small gap between floor and cupboard, but it spins slowly to a stop, just short.

I pick it up again, almost dropping it once more in my shaky haste. The door itself, once unlocked, opens easily, and I pull the Box out from under some test forms placed no doubt with intent to obscure it. I have only taken a few clothes in my bag and there is just room enough for the Box.

I close the cupboard door and switch out the light.

Footsteps thud down the corridor. I climb under the desk with difficulty, the bag on my back jammed against the wood above me. Only eight or so hours earlier I was talking about Father here, feeling guilty that I was betraying him – and to an *umlungu* of all people.

Now, all I feel is fear and the sweat trickling in a cold smelly trail down my neck. I try not to breathe as the door opens and the light flares on. I grip the chisel and a few shards of wood too tightly; blood starts to drip slowly from my right hand.

There is a tired sigh, the light dies and then the door closes. Keys rattle in the lock. I am to be locked in.

More keys rattle and then the man swears; withdrawing a last key, before moving off.

There is a dim light filtering in from the corridor. I release the chisel and wooden splinters, crawl out carefully and stand up. I pluck a tissue from the box on the doctor's desk – the same box he passed to me only hours earlier for my face – and wrap it around my right hand.

With dread, I test the door.

I almost cry with relief when it creaks open. The security man had obviously cursed because he did not have the right keys.

God must be with me.

I scuttle down the corridor like a crab, back pressed against the wall so that I can glance both in front and behind me; but I see no sign of anyone.

The door to the outside opens easily. It feels good to be from an Open Ward, at least.

From there, it is but minutes to the front gate. It is dark enough to sneak past the guard post – the guard himself is occupied with what Father would call the evils of hard pornography. I find it hard not to sneak a look at his TV screen, where a naked man moves on top of a woman, as I crawl underneath the boom and into the bushes in front of the security shed.

Outside. Free.

I text Nombuso and move off quietly towards the main road.

There are sirens in the distance and an owl hoots in a tree ahead of me, freezing the trails of sweat that stripe my body. I wait for Nombuso in the shadows of a jacaranda tree. Pure silence does not exist here either. Inside me, someone growls in response to the hoot of the owl.

I say nothing, though; for only a madman talks to the air.

I doze briefly, but am woken by the throttle of a nearby

motorbike and the dark leathered shape of a woman, silhouetted in unmistakable shape against an orange street lamp. She pulls up in front of me and I see a fluorescent shape circling her cheeks under the helmet – a black, green and gold mini-flag, lined in yellow; there is no way she bought *that* mobile tattoo on the open market.

Why does she flaunt her colours so openly now? Does she wish to take my place in hospital – or perhaps book her space in the grave, still so young?

I rise to greet Nombuso and she hands me a helmet. I climb aboard without question.

I know by now to hold her tight.

Thulani and Gill are waiting in the lounge.

Spread out on the table in front of them are the stripped bones of an automatic rifle, no doubt an AK-47. Thulani is busy clipping in a round of ammunition; another dangles heavily across his right shoulder, giving his body an oddly lopsided look.

Gill is smoking a joint and stands up as we come in.

"You got it, Sib?"

"*Yebo*," I say, swinging the bag off my back, unsure where to put it and somewhat unnerved by the rifle parts strewn in front of me.

Thulani grins at me, "*Mooi gedoen, bra*, as the *boere* would say." He continues to clip the rifle together.

Nombuso looks at the top of the Box when I open the bag. "It's not much to look at, hey."

"How can it be a weapon for us?" I ask. "I know the SB could make good use of it if they ever got hold of this."

"Think about it, Sibusiso," she says, sitting down in front of me, pupils dilated with excitement: "It's a direct route under the skin. If you can connect to anyone, regardless of race, and see how similar we are, how we share so many hopes and dreams, this will negate the skin, making so-called race and colour irrelevant."

I remember her telling me she is studying Soc.Anthrop. too.

"One Box won't go very far," I say doubtfully.

I jump as I hear the rifle *clack*! Thulani has the weapon pieced together and loaded snugly under his arm. "We know people who can make more, given one original," he smiles.

"Who?" I ask, getting out of my chair and moving away from the table. I don't like guns.

Nombuso scoops up my bag with her left hand and silences us with a right index finger held vertically across her lips.

"What?" I ask and she scowls and presses her finger tighter against her lips. Thulani has quietly soft-toed to the back door, rifle cocked and cradled. Gill gets up slowly and I see her eyes are red, her pupils flared. She pulls a pistol from behind her back.

There is no sound; there is nothing to hear. And then it hits me how abnormal that is.

A dog howls nearby, perhaps one of the village strays who occasionally comes in for a beef or chicken bone. Nombuso swings my backpack over her shoulders, scoops up the helmet and grabs my arm, heading for the wide front door.

"Stay low," she says.

She runs crouched, swivels hard right through the door and vaults over the *stoep* wall.

I suddenly hear the baying of bigger and fiercer dogs.

"*Polisie! Hou stil*!" the voice is loud, but distorted, crackling like a whip across my ears as I follow Nombuso over the wall. She has already kicked her bike into action.

I hear the burst of rifle fire from the back door and suddenly she is beside me, pulling me on to her bike. No time for helmets. There is a rapid crackle of gunfire from the darkness of the road, but I don't feel anything, aware only of flashes of light and the snarl of dogs over the roar of Nombuso's bike.

"Hold tight," she snaps and then the bike surges and swings a sharp left unexpectedly, away from the road. There is the rattle of more gunfire and I duck against her, hearing a sharp whine in the air. I smell burning, but Nombuso has twisted the bouncing

105

bike left again and suddenly we are whipping through tall swathes of thick vegetation, along a narrow path... The sugar cane fields at the back of Hope's Folly, I suddenly realise.

I hear no more gunshots, but I see a red-glow in her rear view mirror.

The farmhouse burning.

The motor whines and the wheel spins as Nombuso kicks the ground occasionally, the bike struggling with the mud in the narrow tracks between the fields. A blue light flashes behind us but recedes into the distance; the track is too narrow for a car or van.

The track forks and we swing right. It is hard to see anything at all with a dim half-moon low in the sky. Nombuso is cursing and coaxing her bike and although I am pressed against her, I feel the whip of passing vegetation against my body and the sides of my face. My neck aches, my head forced into an awkward angle by the bulky bag on her back.

She gears down and I see we are in open space by the side of a tarred road.

I feel her body tense, her breath hold, as car lights flash towards... and past us.

She guns the engine again and swings onto the road, then presses the throttle with such force that the bike screams. I lean against her, holding her tightly, burying my head painfully against the bouncing bag, all to stop my lips being pulled open by the savage wind buffeting us.

I lean as she leans and forget all else, my body and mind numb against the roar of the wind.

Finally, the wind and roar lessen and I peer over her shoulder. We are racing along a dark street, shacks on the left, more solid shaped houses on our right. Even in the dull moonlight, the place looks tantalizingly familiar.

Nombuso grinds the bike to a halt and kicks the bike stand down. She sags forward and sighs, exhausted. My body feels locked in shape, frozen, but I eventually manage to let go and stumble off.

By which time a man is coming down the path of the house behind us.

From his shape, a very *big* man!

He stalks past me and helps Nombuso off her bike. I catch a glimpse of his face – tight and serious Numbers. Then they are walking past me and I see Numbers has pulled her arm over his shoulder and is half lifting her. She sags against him as if she is unwell.

I follow. The door opens in front and I see a young child standing there, hanging on the door handle from the inside.

Inside, I recognize Mamma's house, but Numbers and Nombuso have already gone through into one of the side rooms, so I sit and wait in the entrance room. The young boy, as I now see him, comes to sit with me. He must be around eight or nine.

His eyes are wide, his face serious: "Have you been running from the police, Uncle?"

I nod; too tired to do anything else, wondering what Nombuso is doing.

The door opens on the right and Mamma steps though, large and somehow reassuring in her size and presence. I catch a glimpse of Nombuso lying on a bed, bandaged and unmoving.

I moan, but Mamma just holds up a hand: "Nombuso will be fine. She's bleeding from her side, but the bullet grazed her. It has been and gone. As for you, my boy, wipe your face and hand with this."

She passes me a damp cloth which stings my face and right palm. The palm bleeds again, but just a bit.

Numbers comes through: "She sleeps." ('Words' is obviously not his middle name.)

Mamma nods, slips into a room on the left, to return and give me some soup and bread to eat. I wolf it down, hungry and starting to shiver after the night's exertions.

"Thulani and Gill have been killed," Numbers says.

Shocked, I choke down a gulp of hot soup, burning my

throat.

"From police radio?" Mamma asks, turning to him. Numbers nods, watching me.

I put the soup bowl down. I have no more wish to eat. My stomach feels hollow, despite the hot soup and soft bread lining it. The news makes me both sad and shaky. I see Mandla's dead face again. His eye has stopped bleeding, but his body is stiffening, despite all I can do.

Inside me, the Beast bites deep, draining my spirit.

Mamma turns to me: "Eat, my boy."

I shake my head.

She gets up, moves in front of me and then kneels down to bring her face below mine. She balances easily on the balls of her feet, despite her bulk. She smells of sweet milk. Sweet milk – and the bitter curry in a bunny chow.

"Death awaits us all. You must learn the name of the one within you," she says, "The sooner you know who, the easier it will be for you."

I look at her blankly and she sighs. She gets up and pats my head: "Please eat, my boy, you need to sleep before you start another journey in the morning."

"What?" I look up, "Where? What do you mean?"

I cannot go back to hospital; the doctor will know it's me who has taken his Box. Where can I go?

"Zambia," she says, "with the white doctor's Box."

I look at her as if she is mad, but she does not smile, nor does she look like anyone I've seen in the madhouse.

Zambia!

This is a long and hard journey and I need to know why. I hold my stomach to calm the biting Beast within and ask why. Then I ask again.

"Someone there will make copies of the doctor's machine," says Mamma.

I insist on seeing Nombuso.

She is wan and sleeping, her black shirt raised and stretched at the edges around the thick white bandage wrapped around her midriff. I cannot ask her anything, nor wake her. But I can see she is not fit to travel anyway.

I must go alone.

They smile when I tell them and Numbers says he will come with me. Mamma it seems has a back-up bodyguard as well – and another woman who can do her books in the meantime.

"But I have no one who can do everything like you, big man!" Mamma says.

Numbers smiles at Mamma, pleased. As for me, I am very relieved. Numbers looks like a useful man to have on such a dangerous journey, even though he may not talk much.

There will no doubt be time for me to find out the name of the animal – or person – within me.

'Mandla?' I guess, but there is no answer.

Instead, inside me, I sense a deep and perfect silence.

Chapter 10
Martin Moves

Marlene has gone.

I feel angry, *furious,* at Marlene, at Brand, but mostly at myself. It was so fucking obvious – how could I not have seen her for what she was from the outset? Because I didn't want to.

I just didn't want to.

It is hard to get up when the alarm radio kicks in, with news of holiday road deaths and an ANC terrorist cell being destroyed in a farmhouse called 'Hope's Folly' on the outskirts of the city. Two reportedly shot dead in a late night fire-fight... I switch the radio off and cover my head with a pillow.

I'd had my own version of a fire-fight – which had been a batch of self-pitying tears, met only by a brutal put down and more questions from Marlene about the EE Box. At which point I'd lost it and tried to physically throw her out. Small though she was, she'd done some jiu-jitsu thing and left under her own steam, stepping dismissively over my dazed body lying near the front door.

Before crawling back into bed, I'd relocked and gone over the alarms twice and finally put away that picture of Suzette at the Umgeni River Bridge, in an old black photo album in the bedroom cupboard. I'd toyed for a while with the notion of burning the photo, but decided that as it was actually Suzette and *not* Marlene, I needed to treat my memories with discriminatory respect.

File them away; move on.

I'd much rather just lie in bed. I still have a dull headache and am afraid my house is being watched.

But I have that ward round after tea in the Neuro-Clinic, where I have to present the Indian young man with OCD and a fear of cats. He won't get any starting meds or plans for CBT, unless I turn up.

Shit, I wish I could forget about work demands for just one fucking day.

But, whatever happens, I try never to let people down. Not since I left home, anyway.

I dress as casually as I dare, in semi-formal attire, trousers and collared shirt without a tie, draping my hospital ID around my neck. I glance out the window, standing still for moments behind the nudged curtain – but all looks dull and normal, a few sweaty joggers, next-door neighbours on the right heading out on the school run and then on to work. No one I don't recognize – and no lurking Brand or Marlene.

At least, as far as I can see.

My heart pumps at a roadblock into work, but I don't have the energy to avoid it. I pass over my ID book, which a sergeant with a black *snorretjie* grimaces over for a moment before passing it back to me and waving me on.

I drive on, my shirt sticking to my back even though the day's heat has yet to show itself, suddenly aware these things are starting to terrify me – seemingly gone are the days when I would just cluck in annoyance at being stopped.

I arrive at the hospital, swinging my car past the medical superintendent's bay and into the unmarked staff parking section. Mofakane's car is there – a discreetly small BMW, but still a black Be-Em, parked with intent as near to the superintendent's bay as possible. (The hospital is indeed pleased to flaunt one of the first black psychiatrists in South Africa to the outside world.)

Dr. James is already here too, his old Jag a less subtle statement, rusting over the wheels.

Ja, the money's running out, guys – the world is starting to isolate and strangle us. And if not the world, then it's a small bitchy brunette, with a bewildering throw.

Jabu from Jabula Ward is waiting for me at the top of the steps in the Main Building. As always, I smile slightly at the resonance of their names.

But he doesn't look happy in the slightest.

"We've had a runaway, Doctor," he greets me, "But I don't think it's a suicide break."

"Who is it, Jabu?" I ask, still feeling fragile from the night.

"Sibusiso."

"Mchunu?" I stop at the top of the stairs, hesitating.

He nods.

"A pity," I say, "I thought we were making progress. But he's not certifiable – nor did he seem suicidal, as you say." Inwardly, I'm starting to shake, though.

Jabu nods and follows me as I enter the building and turn down the corridor past reception, to my office.

"I just wondered whether you think there may have been a trigger to his suddenly leaving late last night, Doctor?"

I shake my head, keying my door – it takes me several attempts, my hands are trembling hard now: "Sorry, no, he seemed happy we were considering a family meeting."

The key fails to turn, it is already unlocked, and I hope it's just the cleaners again.

"Okay, see you later then, Doctor." He strides off. Despite his bulk, he moves gracefully, silently. (My shoes in contrast, never fail to squeak almost every step of this corridor.)

I push the door open and step inside, sensing wrongness.

I make my way round to the front of the desk. The top-drawer lies open, splintered chips from a broken lock scattered on the floor and inside the drawer. I throw the papers and splinters out, but there is no key.

I turn to look at the test cupboard behind me. It is closed, but the key is in the lock.

For fuck's sake! I jerk the door open and scrabble on the bottom shelf, but know already what I won't find. How can I have been such an idiot? How the fuck could I have been so stupid?

The Box – our EE Box, gone.

Dan will kill me.

Who was it? Not Brand, he'd have picked me up too. It *has to have been...* Sibusiso?

I look under the desk again. Apart from the chisel there are a few sharp, flattish wooden splinters, one marked with a reddish-brown crusty substance that looks like blood. I pick the splinter up gingerly and place it in a small plastic bag that I usually use for bank change.

We've taken blood from Sibusiso – it should be easy to ask the lab to check if this is a match.

I've got an hour or so before the Neuro-Clinic tea and ward-round. I make my way to Jabula Ward.

I have never been here this early. There is no one in the reception area, but I hear singing coming from the room next door.

Singing that raises goose-bumps on my arms, pulling me through, leaving me no choice but to follow the rising and falling of intermingled voices, male and female, staff and patient, in a melodic mix and chant in a language I fail to understand. I cock my head as I push open the door, with a strange feeling that if I just listened hard enough, the meanings would fall into place, the words would etch themselves into my body.

All are in a circle and are dancing too, mixed together, with no sense of division; the words and music bounce and flow between them, like a beautiful but hidden beach ball. There is no instrument but their voices, floating free, spinning around the room and bouncing off me too, wringing tears from my eyes.

The words have fallen now, dropped to the ground with an earthy finality, leaving me hanging and longing for more. The circle breaks, no one has noticed me as yet and I see two staff start plaiting the hair of two women, an older and a younger patient, both in institutional yellow dress and seated now, but looking happy, looking *normal*.

Jabu spots me at last and peels away from the group.

"You're here early, Doctor – what's up?"

"Where has Sibusiso been going for weekend VL, Jabu?"

"He's using a residential college address based where he is studying – why, Doctor?"

I ignore the question. "Who's been signing him out?"

"Last weekend it was a young woman." He raises an eyebrow, no doubt in response to me ignoring his question.

"Can you please find me the address, Jabu? We may need to visit him to make sure he is indeed better and coping with things." (And to find out whether he has stolen my EE Box, the bastard!)

"Sure, Doctor." He turns as a man tugs at his arm, wanting something. Jabu smiles and walks away with him, beefy arm draped over his shoulder. I notice the beaded colours of the ANC on his wrist bracelet – black for the people, green for the land, gold in the Earth – or so I've been told. A risky statement to wear though, they're banned. Or is this a sign the shit is about to *really* hit the fan?

The patients seem relaxed and happy. I wonder whether this early communal hour and more drives the *real* therapeutic change we see eventually, rather than all our pills and formal therapies. I remember Sibusiso did not give credit to our time together either.

I drop the blood sample off at the hospital lab and head back to my office to read up on Patient Reddy, although I shiver as I step into my room. It feels as if nothing is safe from being invaded or violated in my life. My space has been breached both at home and work – and, painfully, inside me as well.

For once I am personally grateful for the box of tissues on my desk.

"Why are you so keen to see this runaway patient, Doctor?" Jabu asks as he waves me left down a road from the passenger seat of my car.

I consider my reply. The lab report was clear – and the laboratory seldom lies. But I can't tell him anything about that. The less people know anything about the theft – and especially *what's* been stolen – the better.

"I've reviewed his notes and think he's a significant suicide risk." Although my eyes are focused on the narrower, unfamiliar road, I can sense the disbelief in the large man next to me.

He says nothing, though I catch a veiled glance out of the corner of my eye.

I relax a bit after skirting the police barrier ahead by taking an even smaller pot-holed road, relatively empty of people – and empty of barricades of burning tyres too. The road swings past box-houses, which billow out of the soil – state housing designed to appease the people – but few people are out walking those straight, sterile pavements, which are marked in neatly controllable squares.

Under Jabu's instruction and chewing on a chocolate bar, I drive on and deeper into the heart of the black township place, where the road runs out and the car bucks across potholes in a sandy track. Tilted corrugated iron shacks sprout alongside the track, winding along a ditch where people are scooping buckets of water with old petrol cans.

I feel frightened, unsure of myself, having crossed a line I have never crossed before.

I am in a real black township.

We stop at a point where other cars and minivan taxis are scrambled on a small field, its grass flattened by traffic and people. I step self-consciously out of the car, very aware of my pale skin here.

"Stay close," says Jabu, "We're taking the back way in; people have been jumpy here since a protest march was crushed recently."

We thread our way past people and taxis, hearing only one muttered 'umlungu' as we reach the chaotic spread of shacks. Some, I note with admiration, are painted carefully in blue or pink, a few are fronted with boxed earth spaces with scraggly plants inside.

"Flowers never last long here – they are a sign of newcomers," says Jabu, "They indicate people who have recently moved from areas where public display is not an invitation to steal."

"Oh," I say.

Once through the scattered cluster of shacks we meet a road that arches into a more built-up residential area. Jabu points at a small tower block: "Student flats for *Fundimiso* College, where Sibusiso was picked up by the mental health outreach team."

"Ah," I say.

Jabu leads the way into the block and checks at the reception desk. Sibusiso is indeed registered at Room number 134.

The clerk rattles something in Zulu at Jabu, who turns to me: "He's not been seen here for a while. We may not be in luck."

I scowl, "Let's check it out anyway."

Jabu shrugs and leads the way down the corridor. Several students drift past with books, some turn to gape at me. Jabu stops outside Room 134 and knocks with loud and beefy knuckles, his wrist now bare.

The door opens. A young man stares at us, dressed in T-shirt and *Bafana* branded slacks; he looks tired and somewhat miserable. There is a further brief but rapid exchange of Zulu before Jabu turns to me. The young man closes the door abruptly.

Jabu shrugs again: "According to Bongani, his roommate Sibusiso has hardly been home since he was hospitalized – he's been spending time with a young woman in his history class called Nombuso..."

"Can we find out where this Nombuso is, then?"

"Probably." He gives me yet another curious look, as if uncertain why I am so intent on tracking a runaway who – to him at least – did not appear to be a serious mental health risk. "Let's ask the clerk at reception. He may have centralized access to student addresses."

We head back down the corridor again. The way is blocked by a gathering group of six or seven black male students, looking sullen and hostile. I drop anxiously behind Jabu's broad back.

This time the exchange of isiZulu is especially rapid, almost hot, although I can only dimly guess at what they might be saying. The group remains knitted together, threatening, a belligerent looking youth at the front taking a lead in the phalanx of students as they step forward slowly, the hint of a *toyi-toyi* dance in their movements.

Jabu turns to me and mutters. "They call me an Uncle Tom for working with a white man, but I'm happy with name calling, as long as it *stays* at that."

He does not move, but I can't rely on him to be a human barricade for me, so I take a deep breath and step around him. The group halts, almost as surprised as Jabu.

But then they step forward again, aggression leaking from their angry faces and clenched fists, halting abruptly as a sharp female voice snaps from behind them; "Keep still, touch no one."

They break open their ranks in the narrow corridor to allow a cropped, striking young woman through – she's short, but muscled, with a bulky midriff that is partly bandaged, I can see a bandage strip at the bottom of her black blouse. She walks with stiff dignity, as if in pain. "What business do you have here?" she asks.

"You know Sibusiso Mchunu?" I ask.

She starts and looks at Jabu, anywhere but at me. She holds her right hand up and splays her fingers. The other students drift away.

Finally, she looks at me, but it's a brief and fleeting glance: "No, I don't know anyone by that name."

Jabu barks a short laugh: "You signed him out of Fort Napier this last weekend."

"I don't know anyone by that name," she repeats stubbornly, glancing behind to the group with an implicit challenge: "Now go."

What can we do? Jabu shrugs his huge shoulders and we start our long slow walk back to my car, before the sun drops too low in the sky.

There are many ways to skin a cat, they say. I think of how else to track Sibusiso and my Box. I also wonder if and when to let Dan know. Jesus, he'll go absolutely *bedonderd* when I tell him, so I won't say anything, not for a while anyhow. Not until I really have to. I run through conversations in my head, but none end happily.

Jabu bumps me with his large hip and I stagger away from him. A man walks between us with a glower, eyes sweeping my face with disdain, before flicking his remote lock to open his taxi minibus door with his left hand.

My stomach tightens when I notice he has a gun in his right hand.

I'm relieved to see my car is still where I left it, all four of its tyres intact.

"Martin," Jabu calls me across the roof of my car, standing by the open passenger door.

"Yes, Jabu?" I say, startled at his use of my first name. It strikes me that he'd done this to get my attention.

"Daydream anymore in a place like this and you are dead meat – *capiche*?" (I wonder if he's watched old gangster or cowboy movies in his youth.)

I swing into the driver's seat, also wondering if Jabu is a Christian or whether he's a follower of a traditional African religion – and whether he's actually shot or killed anyone himself.

I wonder, but I don't ask. The silence feels heavy on our slow, circuitous drive back to the hospital.

It's been a while since I've driven down to Durban.

A full three years since I've driven the ninety K distance with my stomach a cold ball of tension the entire way, seeming to balloon the distance and time into eternity.

Four roadblocks on the way don't help either; the police seem more intense and abrupt, even their veneer of politeness with white people stripped bare. My breath catches each time they look at my ID book, in case Brand is still after me and has alerted the police, but my ID is handed back with a cursory grunt each time, their search of my car revealing nothing except scraps of Lunch and Tex bar chocolate wrappings and a few battered editions of the South African Journal of Psychology.

By the time I hit the outskirts of Durban, my stomach is tied in a knot so tight it feels as if I'm on the verge of vomiting. The distant sparkle of the Indian Ocean soothes the stomach subtly, helping me breathe somewhat easier as I swing across the Umgeni River and begin the quick turns that take me to my parent's barricaded home in Durban North.

I pull up outside the mechanised white gate, fighting the impulse to reverse and get the hell out of here.

The number on the gate is a cute and curlicued blue '33', a contrast to high walls that look like they host a fully manned watch-tower behind them – complete with razor wire and surveillance cameras. Judging from the taut fist that tugs at my innards, there may just as well be a harsh and prison-like environment waiting within.

The gate rolls open. I have been observed.

I have to remind myself that it's just my parents who await me. Nothing nasty, nothing terrible – just my own flesh and blood – and, after all, he *is* my father.

I creep up a driveway flanked by hydrangea bushes, offering up a prayer to a God I no longer believe in.

I don't recognise her at first – a slightly bent woman with a forceful swagger struts across the paved walkway from the house to meet me. I step out of the car and fall into her arms. She smells slightly of nutmeg and almond essence. Old memories of cake and *koeksisters* are sparked by her smell and her initially slightly hesitant, but finally firm, hug.

"Hi, Ma," I say, "How are you?"

We look at each other and she keeps a firm grip on my elbows. She's quite a bit greyer, and has chosen not to hide it. Her black-grey hair is bobbed onto the stiff collars of her frilly pink blouse, tucked into her long grey skirt that drops down to square and sensible brown shoes. Always sensible is Ma – but God, suddenly so *old*.

"You've gone plump, Marty," she says, with a bluntness that rolls back the years.

"Yes, Ma," I say, with a resignation that anticipates yet another conflict ridden visit.

But still I remember Sibusiso's words – he'd told me he was scared, but he needed to put things right with his father and insisted I make the family appointment. When I asked why, he just said: 'He's my father.'

Physician, heal thyself.

Ma leads me up the pathway towards the door, past familiar imported roses and flowers alien to the gathering wet heat of a Durban summer day. The door is open and she pulls me in to the cold chill of a dark and severe air-conned house, sitting room and lounge saturated with dark woods and lace curtains and table cloths, old pictures of people and places that track and anchor our families past and future; stiff, respectful, good Afrikaner ancestral *volk* who stare at you from pictures that both fade and breathe with residual life and expectation. I remember it all, yet it feels so terribly alien, so distant.

The air is humid and thick with expectations I cannot fulfil – a good and devout Afrikaner wife who anticipates and echoes my thoughts, babies who do likewise and me being both a stern father and a caring son, doing my part for my elders. Staying close and caring for his parents as an only son should do. Attending the local NG *Kerk* with them on Sundays, doing some diligent and respected law work during the week, work which reinforces the justness of the apartheid system.

This was a mistake. I should leave. But I suddenly notice the old man seated in the big rocking chair, facing out the window, with a dull look on his face.

Jesus. I mean – *liewe* God! – *Pa* has aged much more than *Ma* has. He's now completely bald with liver spots and seems to have bent into the shape of the rocking chair. He's dressed in restrained brown shirt and trousers – but looks at me now, with eyes that sharpen with each passing second.

"Hello, my boy." His voice is much more muscular than his body appears and he makes an attempt to stand. Ma helps him up and he holds out a shaky right hand.

I grip it fearfully and am surprised at the sudden painful snap of his sinewy hand. He grins then, in that old self-assured and cocky way, a smile that asserts he is leading the way on the Only True Way to Life. A retired barrister, I had been unable to reason with him three years ago – about who I was and what I wanted – and I had left, vowing never to return, closing my ears and heart.

Sometimes it takes more effort to keep something closed, than to try and open it again.

"Sit, my boy," he gestures me to the couch, so I take the chair. Ma retires to the kitchen to potter with cakes and tea.

He folds his body back down into the rocking chair and I stare at his profile as he rocks backwards and forwards, again not getting a prolonged and clear face to face view of who he actually is.

What I would give to have my EE box here, to clip and connect the air between us!

"How is work?" he asks eventually, as Ma brings in a tray draped with lace and two mugs and a pile of *koeksisters*.

I shake my head as she offers me the sweetmeats: "Aren't I too fat to risk one of those?" I regret it immediately, my voice sounding harsher than I'd meant.

Her face crumples briefly and I suddenly see years of hurt layered under her skin. It hits me then – there is an old and familiar path of argument and pain that is easily trodden – or there are attempts to find new roads, pot-holed and empty, scary and threatening, leading past shacks and houses, to new spaces, new people.

I must take a new and uncertain road, with or without my

Box, if I am going to find change, something, anything worthwhile.

I stand up and take the tray from her: "Sorry, Ma, that was rude of me. You sit please and I'll get you something to drink. What would you like?"

She looks at me, too hurt to sit.

It is then that I remember she likes her tea with hot milk and one sugar. So I place the tray on the tablecloth and make my way into the kitchen, overwhelmed with flashbacks of being shorter, younger and waiting to lick out the mixing bowl of chocolate icing. I wait for nothing now, but pour another mug of tea and heat some milk in the microwave.

It pings at me after a minute and by the time I walk through, mug in hand, Ma is seated in the chair I have vacated. She looks at me askance, as if unsure of me, but I take the mug over to her and give it to her first. "Here you go, Ma – and thank you."

She takes the mug and looks up at me with an uncertain smile.

But all I see is an empty chair; all I feel is the burn of what seems like a never-ending seep of grief.

I choke.

Ma stands in concern, but she seems little more than a ghost, wafting up from a cold and empty chair.

Her hands are warm though, clutching anxiously at my left arm, almost upsetting my tray.

Why had I thought for a panicked moment that she was gone, dead?

Oddly, I bow, carefully placing the tray down.

"God be with you, Mother."

I weep as she kisses my cheek, her breath musty and hot in my nostrils.

Pa looks up as I offer him a *koeksister* with his black tea, seemingly unaware of anything unusual. He hesitates for a moment and then takes it with a mumbled '*dankie*'.

Ma watches me, but with her head cocked in concern.

I sit on the couch and we sip our tea in silence.

My tears have frozen on my face; I know Sibusiso's pain flickers inside me; my life is no longer fully mine.

"How have things been with you, my boy?" Pa puts his mug down on the chair – Ma has finally started to eat her own *koeksister*. I smile and fill them in briefly about life and work, but it is an easy decision to leave out the bit about the EE machine and the Security Police. Being with family is a constant show and hide, but this time I show more than usual.

So too, I feel more respect than is usual.

I ask them how they are in return and hear a bit about seasonal planting and their garden, what goes on at church and the dire state of the country.

Somehow, the talk is easier than it was three years ago, shifting through old and new subjects, faltering over hot topics, but no one choosing to enflame these. It's as if we all have a renewed sense of each other and are tacitly trying to build new and firmer bridges of communication for each other. For Pa, he seems to have mellowed with the bend of his back and the emptying of his scalp. For me, I think perhaps my sense of others has been sharpened by the Box – and I can almost swear I hear Sibusiso's breath inside me.

Still, the EE Box itself is not a necessary thing. Sometimes words and good will alone travel a long way. We even finish talking with the hint of a smile hovering between us.

They ask me if I will stay for the night. I thank them, but decline, realizing good will takes time and enduring energy to build and needs careful, constant nurturing. Perhaps tomorrow will be different anyway, back to old and well-carved paths of pain and disappointment.

I will take what I have, while it still buds inside me.

I have brought my costume and towel, perhaps in order to wash off a bitter visit in the warm and rough waves of Durban North Beach. This time I will just bodysurf in the water, flirting with dolphins and not sharks, I hope – or maybe there will just be other (white) swimmers.

Then, finally, I will return home and think of a new way to find Sibusiso and my EE Box.

As they open the gate for me and I cruise down the driveway, I know it will be much less than three years before I come back next time.

In the rear-view mirror I catch a glimpse of the gate closing on my parents, standing together, arm in arm. Almost forty-five years together, I remember, turning down to the beach, my spirits soaring as the sound of the surf builds in my ears, my right arm burning in the sun as I tap the roof of my car to the banned hip-hop beat of Gil Scott-Heron's 'The Revolution Will Not Be Televised.'

Chapter 11
Sibusiso in Zambia

Ladysmith is the furthest I have been from Underberg, the place of my birth.

I went with *tata* once, when the *baas* drove us up for a cattle show, as he wanted to ask Father what he thought of some of the cattle he was hoping to buy. Father insisted I come too, the eldest son, as he thought I was ready to learn some cattle lore from them.

We travelled in the back of the *baas's bakkie* of course, through the worst of the day's heat, but Father gave me the biggest sips from the water bottle he had brought.

The *baas* believes we do not get sunburnt because we are black. Father had a light cloth he covered us with when the sun baked the most. I'm still burnt sore and bored stiff at the cattle show though – Ladysmith itself seemed like a dull and dusty town and the white people seemed even ruder than usual; I heard the word 'kaffir' thrown around a good deal more than I was used to.

Father loved it, though – cattle were in his blood, he has always been a real umZulu. As for me, I pretended I loved cows as much as I could, as they trailed around a large ring on show, but I was constantly longing to go home and learn of other things at school, like history, geography and mathematics.

From geography, I learned Ladysmith was two hundred and fifty kilometres from home. That seemed a long, long way to have travelled indeed, something to boast about at school, although a few claimed to have gone further than me. On a few maps of Africa I'd seen, however, the continent had stretched above us for thousands and thousands of kilometres; over fifty countries, all ruled by black people, almost all men – except for our land, defiantly white South Africa.

Zambia itself had seemed especially important. Although we were not taught so formally, we all knew amongst ourselves that some of our exiled leaders were there: Mbeki, the son, Zuma, and Hani himself, the stuff of legend, military chief, dodger of bombs.

Yes, others were banned or in hiding or on Robben Island – but some at least were free in Lusaka, the capital of a black African country – managing itself fine off the back of large copper sales, mainly to the Russians and Chinese.

And now I am on my way there myself.

This time it would be thousands of kays, not hundreds.

But only in the slowest and most uncomfortable way – so here I lie, on the bottom of a truck carrying bags of polystyrene bubbles used as packaging fillers, down to Durban and the harbour. The routes through the Mozambique border have apparently been sealed by the South African army, with inside info from the SB. Zimbabwe, of course is a no-go zone, with Mugabe selling out to his white Southern neighbours, who'd squeezed his trade lifelines mercilessly until he'd caved in.

This is a completely new way, so Mamma had told me – we hoped the SA naval patrols were less vigilant on the sea route up to Maputo, past Richard's Bay, past Pondoland, into foreign waters, where a sprightly Samora Machel stays president.

Right now, though, the sea seems a long way off. The Durban road is better than most, but I feel every bounce bruises my backbone – and although the bags are light and loose and bounce around, they still seem to suck the air from the back of the truck, so that I gasp for breath, although I know that it is in my head. I look over to Numbers, occasionally losing sight of him behind tumbling bags; but he lies quietly, as if dead, head propped underneath a heavier bag that seems to act like a pillow. I don't know how he can look so comfortable, as the bag includes the doctor's Thought Box.

I have a similar bag for my head – its heaviness comes from accumulated gifts and letters for relatives in Zambia, but to me it pokes and pricks my head in new and discomfiting ways, with each jolt and jar of the truck.

We are stopped and twice the doors at the back are opened and I lie, panicking about the loudness of my held breath. I fail to see Numbers as the bags have settled over our bodies and faces, so I force myself to lie quietly and start breathing slowly and silently, before my lungs explode, compromising us. The truck has sagged under the weight of someone stepping inside, followed by a rummaging sound, and bags have bounced around us, but thankfully not away from us. Twice the truck bounces up again, as someone steps off and the door slams and the truck revs up again, matching my racing heart.

The third stop follows after an interminable range of sways and bumps, as if we have left the main road. This time the back door opens and the whistle of 'all clear' slices through the bags on our wet faces. I slap the bags away, gulping air with relief, feeling like I've sweated the entire Indian Ocean out of my body on the journey. Numbers hauls me to my feet with a powerful right arm, seemingly none the worse for wear, although masking his mouth with his left hand as he yawns. I have the idea this is far from his first time on such a trip.

The driver is a tall, gangly Indian man, who is relatively fluent in isiZulu. (Numbers had told me he was a recent recruit through the CDF, the recently banned Combined Democratic Front.) He does not want to hang around, though.

"My number plate is still clean to the cops, so I'm going to have to drive like fuck to get my delivery in, before any eyebrows are raised. *Salani kale.*"

He runs around to the front of the truck, without waiting for us to reply.

I double over from cramps in my legs, but Numbers pulls me clear from the road, which is part tarred and potted, part gravel. The truck spins away in a spray of stone and I yelp as one catches me on the shin.

I stand up and think – what – the – hell?

The road winds close to the coast and we are in a small

isolated bay, waves washing in with small 'whooshes', which I'd not heard over the engine. The cove is rocky, bleak and not a place to swim it seems, shark-warning sign staked into the ground near what looks like the easiest route into the sea. The sky is darkening as dusk settles in and I see no one else around.

My uncle took us once to the black beach south of Durban, but I'd never made it in further than my ankles. But Numbers strides towards the beach, bag under arm, waving me to follow on behind. I wonder whether he had ever been able to learn to swim, he certainly seems fearless enough.

I swing the bag onto my back via the straps and hobble over the rocks, much more slowly and cautiously behind Numbers, who bounds around the cove to make the way towards a prominent boulder far out on the right.

I keep a respectful eye on the sea and my feet, as the bag swings a scary degree of uncertainty into my balance. My legs are also tingling with their lengthy inactivity, but at least my sweaty body is drying in the day's dying heat. I treat each rock with separate respect.

The last boulder is huge, but Numbers reaches down to grab my arms and pull me on top, my feet scrabbling briefly on its slippery side surface. There is a wide, flatter surface on top, on which a green plastic tarpaulin has been laid, with a torch, set of binoculars and several crumbling sandwiches and bottle of water.

"Fancy a picnic, Sibusiso?" he grins at me.

I sit cross-legged and swig the water first, before devouring the beef sandwich – manna from heaven.

Numbers sits long-legged facing the sea, scouring the horizon with his binoculars. I want to ask whether I can have his sandwich too, but know better than to do so. As the eldest son, I have also known how to sleep with a rumbling belly when required.

"Do you have a cell phone?" he asks me, swinging left with his binoculars again, staring at the horizon. It is getting too dark to see and I feel my fear rising, even though the sea seems to be falling away.

"Yes," I say, hauling it out of my pocket and switching it on.

Numbers snatches it from me with his left hand, holding his binoculars steady with his right hand, cursing briefly. With a flick of his wrist, he flings my phone into the sea.

"Hey!" I shout, appalled. It had been my eighteenth birthday present from my father.

"Sorry, boy," he says, out of the side of his mouth, "the *boere* no doubt have a lock on your calls. That phone is not only useless, but it's dangerous."

I am still upset and angry. We have been taught to throw nothing away.

"Ahhhh...." he puts the binoculars down and picks up the torch, standing quickly with the surety of a fit man. With one hand he shields the torch, flashing it towards the ocean.

I strain my eyes, but see nothing in the deep gloom.

Then I hear it: a slight engine sound, a flickering light in the darkness. Something is coming towards us and it's obviously not a shark.

Numbers pulls the tarpaulin up and crumples it into his big bag, along with the binoculars. He hands me the sandwich. "Eat well, boy, we still have a very long way to go."

I stand to eat, bag on my back, peering into the darkness. Numbers stands alongside me, flashing into the night. Then he steadies his right hand, focusing the beam on the sea in front of us. A shape emerges from the darkness, a small rowing boat with one person rowing, the boat bouncing on the surging of the sea, passing in and out of the torch's light.

"It's too risky bringing the main boat in close. Give me your bag."

I do so and he gives me the torch to hold: "Try and keep it on the boat."

This proves harder than it sounds; although the man at the oars seems skilled at stabilizing the boat, it still slides across the swell of the sea. I track it as best as I can, it's now only several metres away and Numbers slings my bag in successfully.

"Now for the hard part," he says, slinging his own large bag off his back.

"Brother!" he shouts to the oarsman struggling in the boat, "I need you to catch this one, it's very valuable and we need nothing to break inside."

The man in the boat shouts something back and Numbers laughs.

"Hold the torch steady, Sibusiso," he barks to me and throws – just as the man releases his oars to turn towards us. The man holds out his arms and the boat swings out of view.

"Fuck!" Numbers shouts and I swing the torch to try and locate the boat; afraid it has slipped onto the rocks, although I have heard nothing.

I can't find it, but a man's voice calls out of the darkness. "I am here. I told you not to doubt me, Numbers, I told you I am a top slip fielder for the Mandela Eleven cricket team."

Numbers laughs again, just as I locate the boat slipping in closer to us – the man is back at his oars, two bulging bags at the front of his boat.

Numbers turns to me: "How good is your long jump?"

"What?" I ask dumbly.

He sighs: "Can you swim?"

"What?" I repeat.

"Never mind," he says, throwing the torch into the boat. With one fluid motion, I feel him sweep my legs from under me with his own leg and then I am sliding down the rock towards the seething sea.

I scream, but something has my shirt in its grasp. I hit the water with a shock and scrabble at it, dark bubbles in front of me and I am choking on salty wetness. The water is warm, thank God, and I gasp, but this time I take in air and not water, somehow my face is above the waves.

Something is thrusting me upwards and then I feel strong arms pulling me over a hard surface and I roll inside a flat wooden space, coughing. A shape sprays alongside the boat and hangs on, the boat lurches and dips as the shape rears up and rolls over, bumping heavily into me. I feel myself thrown against a bag at what must be the front of the boat, but it yields under me, no fragile or sharp surfaces inside.

Oars splash and I continue to cough water out of my mouth. Above me, an even larger shape looms out of the darkness, dimly lit, a chugging boat with taller sides. A light flashes and I see ropes tumbling down its side.

We sway alongside and I see in the flashes of torchlight that it is a rope ladder.

"Climb!" says Numbers next to me.

This time I say nothing, but stagger to my feet and wait until the boat lurches close enough. I lean across, grab the ladder with both hands and swing a foot up onto a ropy step. For several moments I swing against the larger boat, banging my elbow against the side of the larger boat, my feet in a tangle.

Then, slowly but steadily, I climb the ladder.

"*This*, I know how to do," I shout back down into the darkness.

Numbers' deep roll of laughter follows me up the swinging ladder.

The captain greets us as we climb aboard. He is a white man, I notice with shock, but his accent is thick, strange and definitely not South African. Still, he does not wait for us to dry and no one else offers us anything.

"Go below and stay there – Dimitri will show you the bunk you must share. You will wash up after all meals. We head now into ...ahhhh, non-territorial waters... if we are boarded, we give you up, without questions being asked, having rescued you miles out to sea."

He turns, thick jersey partially hidden by shiny full-length overall. He clumps up a flight of steps in black gumboots, I think, although it's hard to gauge colour in the dimmed ship's lights. I'd only guessed he was the captain by virtue of him standing in the foreground, three other white men hanging behind him – that, and the fact that he wore a hat that looked a bit like Captain Haddock in a *Tintin* comic I'd read from the traveling township library.

They – and everything around us – reek of fish.

"A Russian fishing vessel," says Numbers in my ear.

"He might as well have been South African," I mutter.

Dimitri, I presume – a small wiry man with a blank, pockmarked face, black bushy hair and beard – gestures us towards steps leading downward into the boat. The other men are winching the rowing boat aboard and I hear the thump of someone landing on the deck behind us.

But I am being jostled ahead by Dimitri, who holds my right elbow in a tight grip, as I stumble against the sway of the ship. At least the wooden railings leading down into the murky bowels of the ship enable me to shuffle downwards without falling, given I grip tightly and walk sideways like a crab. Dimitri himself dances ahead of me, needing no grip, turning to look at me occasionally and with undisguised impatience.

I do have vague misgivings on the way down, remembering progressive teachers inserting the Atlantic slave trade illegally into their teachings on (white) South African history. But Numbers breathes reassuringly behind me, so I keep moving, albeit at a painfully slow creep.

The steps bottom out into a narrow corridor and Dimitri heads down what seems to be the smelliest side, although it's hard to be sure, as *everything* stinks – and I am starting to feel decidedly queasy. He stops and opens a small door to his right, waving me in, grinning.

I've yet to trust a white man's smile – even Dr. van Deventer's smile was not always reassuring. I step inside, but only because I can feel the pressure of Numbers' presence hovering powerfully behind me. He follows me in, as does the third man – almost inconceivably, given the tiny size of the room.

It looks like a room for lost and missing equipment: bits and pieces of rope, broken metal, tools... and a fishing net, splayed across the small floor. Behind us, the door closes. "See you for – morning meal," comes the muffled and diminishing shout of a receding Dimitri.

I lean against the far wall, feet tangling in the net, but somehow manage to turn to look at the others. Numbers is so big, dominating the room to such an extent, that at first I don't see the much smaller man. He's standing a bit behind Numbers and is only armpit height to him, but his chest and arms look as thick as a tree. It is hard to see him in the dimmed light dropping from lighted vents around the room, but he seems sure of himself and the space around him.

"Xolile," he greets me, leaning forward to handshake, thumb grip, palm, and thumb grip, "Welcome aboard, cousin." He's *umXhosa*, but I don't hold that against him, he was so good with his oars.

Numbers stretches and the room shrinks even more. "The fishing net's our bed, Sibusiso," he says," So try not to roll too much; otherwise they may think you're a real catch."

Xolile laughs and reaches behind him: "And guess what's for breakfast, lunch and supper."

My stomach lurches with the boat but Xolile has the bucket in front of my face. I spew with shame, sagging to my haunches as my feet are trapped in the net. Xolile lowers the bucket to keep pace with my collapse.

This is going to be a *long* trip.

I *hate* fish.

It's actually a shorter trip than I'd feared. The ship had powerful motors and once fully out at sea it went like a mad horse, bouncing across the water.

But my stomach bounced too and I was unable to keep any food down. I had one change of clothing in my bag, but everything turned quickly into a fishy smell.

My mind cheered when we finally saw shore, the sprawling smeared shape of a coastal city emerging ahead of us. Maputo, Numbers told me. Both he and Xolile had to support me off the boat, though, I was so weak and sick.

Then there was the train ride – that took longer than I'd hoped, rattling across a great distance, swaying too, but less aggressively. So my stomach grew stronger and I was able to eat bits of chicken and bread; Numbers had a small wad of foreign currency in his bag. We slept in the cabin, sitting up and propped against each other. There were three other Mozambiquans opposite us, two young men and a woman and they looked smartly dressed compared to us, looking down their noses at us and speaking a funny language.

"Portuguese." Numbers whispers to me as it darkens yet again outside.

He sleeps with a rigid grip around his bag. Mine, I use as a pillow.

I watch Africa shift slowly around me: town, scrubland, thin forest – denuded by Renamo from the Civil War, Numbers tells me. Town, forest, grassland... and two men in uniform enter our cabin, but they are black men.

Still, my stomach tightens, but they smile as they stamp papers Numbers holds out to them.

"Welcome to Zambia," says one in English, as he leaves the cabin.

And so it is that we arrive in a town, a fairly big one at that, rattling for quite a while past buildings before we grind to a slow halt.

Numbers stands up as do the other passengers opposite us. "And now, welcome to Lusaka."

I am both relieved and excited.

We step off the train and people push past us, all certain of where they are going. Hawkers stride the platform, with fruit, meat and vid-phones.

I look around. I do not see a white face.

Numbers pulls a cell-phone from his pocket and switches it on.

"How have you kept yours?" I ask, angry.

He shrugs and examines a text. "Sorry, my boy, I had to be sure you didn't use it in a moment of weakness."

Boy. Weakness. My anger rises even more. The long miles have worn all of our relationships into a thin thread of bare tolerance.

We are jostled again and Xolile guides us to the 'Lusaka' metal sign, where the crowd is thinner. Our train pulls out, heading back towards Mozambique.

Numbers examines his phone again and gives a bark of surprise. "Plans have changed," he says.

"How?" asks Xolile. Our words with each other have become short, sharp and extremely to the point. (Xolile has given up talking cricket with me, as I'm strictly a football fan, my team being the Buccaneers, although I have never been to Orlando.)

Numbers gestures up the platform.

At first all I see is a thronging mass of people, some travellers, some new hawkers with bags of cheap jewellery, and many people just standing and talking amongst each other, some smoking. Then I see a paler man walking towards us purposefully, neatly dressed in a creamy yellow shirt and slacks, white floppy sun-hat as shade against the building heat of the day.

But he is not white. Well, not quite.

"The Russians are withdrawing overt support from us while negotiating peace with the Americans," says Numbers. "The Chinese have registered their interest in the box."

The man is slight and of medium height with black hair peeping out from under his sun-hat. I feel dirty and smelly – and slightly ashamed of my appearance, he is so neat.

He bows.

His English is fluent, clipped and precise, perhaps better than mine.

"Welcome, gentleman, I have a car for you. The Chinese

government is interested in supporting you – that is, if you have the, uh, electronic Box?"

Numbers pats the bag he wears on his chest protectively; it expands his bulk forward so that I feel small, superfluous, an inconsequential hanger on.

"Good," says the man, "Chung Li is my name."

He shakes hands Western style, bowing at each of us in turn as we say our names.

"Good to meet you," he says: "Now let me take you to somewhere more comfortable. The place also has a bath."

We follow him and I wonder briefly whether Chung Li has also mastered the white man's art of subtle, as well as overt, hint and denigration.

But a bath sounds good. *Very* good. I want to scrub away the fish, which feels as if it has sunk beneath my very skin.

The house is comfortable. Much more comfortable than anything I have lived in. It even has air conditioning – we watch as the black servant tunes the system so that it cools the heat out of the day's air. The servant speaks Bemba and is reluctant to use English; although I have no doubt he is practised at the art of seeming to understand much less than he really does.

And the bath is indeed wonderful – I lie for over an hour, soaking my bruises, cuts and, most of all, the enduring stench of fish, off my skin. Numbers bangs on the door eventually and I give the bath up reluctantly, but am delighted to find new clean clothes in a whole room designated for me. On the bed lie yellow slacks, underpants and shirt, so I wonder if it is indeed part of a uniform.

We eat well, not Chinese, but grilled chicken and the local version of *samp*. Along with crunchy green beans, it feels as if the meal has dropped down from heaven.

But a black man still serves the food, so I'm glad it's just a simile and not how heaven may actually operate – at least, so I hope. I manage a smile at my own joke, having remembered my

English classes. For the first time in the better part of three days we have travelled, I relax.

There is little conversation, for we are too busy enjoying the food. Our host calls us aside afterwards, though.

"Time to test the goods," he says.

He takes us to a quiet room deep in the heart of his huge house, where there are no windows – and the walls themselves seem to have been hushed. By comparison to the lushness of the rest of the house, it is a bare room indeed, with a few chairs, a table and nothing hanging off the walls. Even the floor seems to be silenced wood.

I wonder what purpose this room normally serves, but Numbers already has Dr. Van Deventer's Box out on the table. He leaves me to clip the caps in, as I remember the doctor doing. The Box smells a bit of fish, although perhaps that's just my memory of our arduous journey intruding.

Our host sits opposite me.

"I read you," he says eagerly.

I hesitate. He gestures impatiently: "I must read you to be sure it works. You will not be able to read me."

I am not sure if he means will not, cannot, or should not.

Numbers signs at me to proceed. Xolile slumps against a wall, looking on with disinterest, as if his life revolves around rowing, cricket and illegally crossing international borders.

I place the caps – first on my head and then on Chung Li's. His hair is soft and short, easy to manage.

He pushes a pad and pen my way. "Write down in English what you intend to imagine and then fold the sheet so I see nothing."

I write, noticing he has closed his eyes. I fold the sheet over twice to make sure he sees nothing.

He opens his eyes: "Now focus on one specific image in your mind. Make it as simple and clear as possible."

I switch the machine to export from my cap and close my eyes, concentrating hard. After a minute or so, I open my eyes.

Chung Li's eyes are closed, but he is smiling.

I switch the machine off and unclip my cap.

He opens his eyes but does not bother reaching for the paper. "I too, have fished with my father," he says.

Homemade rod, I think, tears coming to my eyes, and we caught nothing.

Tata.

Chung Li smiles again and looks across to Numbers. "We will take the Box and remunerate your organization well. We will also do as you ask about the additional supplies."

Numbers steps forward and rubs his huge hands together: "How long?"

"Two days at most."

I see Numbers jerk with surprise.

Chung Li unclips his cap and stands, hand outstretched for a sealing handshake. "We have been investigating this sort of technology independently ourselves and are almost there. We have most of the resources and circuits nearby and already share much with this continent; and we're always looking for ways to simplify our uh… *communications.* The locals can be so – what is the word the English use – *inscrutable?*"

I am puzzled by his last word, although Xolile barks a short laugh. Chung Li smiles and I wonder how much is shared, how much is bought, how much is taken.

Numbers shakes hands on the deal and I look across at Xolile. This looks like we have several more days of hearing the differences between a straight versus cover drive then – with good food and a bed thrown in.

We've already had a hack at a borrowed football in the big back garden.

I can see why he's so fond of cricket – Xolile's shit at football.

But he's an amazing wizard on a computer – a natural, he says – showing me in his room how he can programme a search and publish Internet engine, gathering rapid and weighty anti-apartheid knowledge from all sources of the world, irrespective of language *or* symbol.

He clicks a button and smiles. "I just sent this shit-load of stuff direct, untraceable, to the Department of Tourism in Pretoria."

Sure, Xolile may be rubbish at football.

Still, he's nicer than Numbers.

The night before we leave I approach Numbers, asking whether I can stay, to further my political education in a country where black people actually rule.

"No," he says, without bothering to look at me. I follow his gaze to the TV screen in his room. His long body sinks deep into the bed.

It looks like an action movie, although it is indeed strange to see only black actors on screen.

Then he turns to me, "Nollywood; the Nigerians know how to make fucking good movies. Smooth, huh, brother?"

"Why can't I stay here?" I will not let him distract me.

He clucks his tongue with impatience. "Maybe next time. Not now. You're the only one who's seen how this Box works. We need you back there."

He waves me away.

I leave his room, to the sound of gunfire in my ears.

Chapter 12
Martin Crosses Boundaries

Being white has many advantages.

It takes only a few phone-calls after work from my hospital office to the *Fundimiso* College hierarchy to gain the information I want. I know my voice is recognized as white, my Afrikaner accent sufficiently soft to perhaps even be mistaken for an English white – whatever, the rector and admin staff give me the information I'm after, particularly as I emphasize my doctoral status.

In the space of a few phone calls I have the addresses of Nombuso and a teacher who has adopted a mentor role towards Nombuso and who has also taught Sibusiso. She is a history teacher, a Dr. Wadwalla, resident in Northdale. It must be the same woman who spoke at that PsychSoc meeting.

I also learn that Sibusiso has failed to attend classes, as he has also failed to return to hospital. It is not unusual for people to abscond at the hospital and those not certified seldom get chased. I will need to be discreet about why *this* one, in case it comes to anyone's attention. Dr. James, old though he is, watches me at times through slitted eyes.

I ponder the little I know, wondering whether to search the web for more information on all three people from *Fundimiso* College. I send out preliminary searches on each of their names, but get very little in return, just a standard reply to all: 'censored'. Fuck! It's a castrated local web indeed. Not only is the Internet firewalled around South Africa, they're patrolled by SAP spybots and carved into smaller segregated information fiefdoms by the specific company which manages – and regulates – your access. In Fort Napier's case, it's the Health Insurance giant, GETWELL-KWIK.CO.ZA.

I stare at the empty search screen results for Nombuso

Ngena; Sibusiso Mchunu and Fariedah Wadwalla. 'You need insurance against Type-II diabetes; apply now and win an exclusive free golf lesson at Durban Country Club.' I wonder which bloody company sold my details to GWK.

The screen flashes red. VIRUS ALERT!

I run the anti-viral programme, but it switches itself off halfway through and I stare with dread at the screen: 'Your IP address has been noted by the South African Police. We will contact you in due course. Have a nice day!'

I download EE recordings onto a Mem-disc, deleting it from the hard drive and pocketing the disc securely.

I switch off the machine and lean back, cursing again. What the hell have you been up to, Sibusiso? And where's my fucking Box? And now this…

I toy with the idea of swapping machines with Dr. James – perhaps I can interchange all the files completely, enough to fool the police? A desperately stupid ploy indeed – I see the ID scratch marks on the computer casing and remember it's linked to both our IP address and staff names. Whatever I do, all data will still point to me.

There is one phone call I need to make – and I do so quickly.

I stand up and stretch; body taut with gloomy fear. There seems to be a noose tightening around me, as if that bullet I threw off Umgeni Bridge has gained a boomerang life of its own. The space between my shoulder blades feels itchy, but I am too fat and lack the suppleness to get anywhere near scratching it.

I look down at my broken drawer. Dan will no doubt phone soon as well, to find out how the new Box works. I feel frozen by growing terror, trapped by events, stuck in a web from which there is no escape.

But then I remember how I got Sibusiso to move when I first met him – and now he's moved away and beyond me, to somewhere I don't know. As for me, I know suddenly I need to move too – and fast; that unmarked bullet swells in my mind now. Pa had always told me a moving target is hardest to hit, *and* he'd given me a little spontaneous wave when I'd left him and Ma in Durban – a small hand gesture, but one I hadn't seen for many years, hinting at an invitation back.

It's not the right time, though, not now, not until – and if – I can get this shit sorted out and my Box back. To do that, I need to *move*.

The spaces I can move have also expanded, so come on, Martin; it's not all a contracting net. But where should I go *now*?

My door is open, but a nurse knocks. I can tell it is a nurse because I can see his blue uniform; his muscular black wrist, his exposed ANC bracelet. He no longer hides himself from me; there's some show of trust, it seems.

"Come in, Jabu," I say.

He peers around the door without stepping inside. "There's a Special Branch agent, Doctor, here on site. A contact saw him coming in and alerted me – I got to the medical superintendent's office and caught a snatch of conversation from his office. They want you."

"Oh," I say, frozen in place again.

He steps into the office and without warning swings his hip into me. I stagger against the desk, shocked and shaken.

He lifts a finger at me: "Remember what I told you in *Imbali*, Martin? Well, it's time to stop dreaming here too – and you'd better come in my car, because they have someone watching the gate with an alert on your car."

"Why would you help me?"

"The enemy of my enemy... Now stop; pick up your bag, and let's *hamba*!"

Jabu's heels squeak as he leaves the room. I hesitate, surely it's just delaying the inevitable, they will get me in the end – but if there is no evidence of the second Box, they can't nail me with anything, surely? Or have they watched us and tracked our local workers on the new Box? If so, we're screwed.

Jabu steps back into the room without any warning noise

from his shoes – and there is a snarl on his face. He towers over me but does not touch me again. He takes a deep breath and then calms his features, before speaking, rapidly.

"You have a choice, Martin: come with me and do something positive for everyone in this country, or stay here and wait for them to come and nail you for whatever you may or may not have done. Even if they don't get you, you stay now, odds are you're going to end up hiding away and changing *nothing*. I'm giving you thirty seconds and that's it..." He takes a deep breath after such a long speech and taps his watch.

I always need to know where I am going. "Where?"

"Northdale."

"Wadwalla?"

He smiles, "Fifteen seconds."

But I'm already out the door.

I've known it since Brand's first invasion of my home.

Being white carries no ultimate guarantees either.

I feel both frightened and small, crouching low on the back seat of Jabu's car, as we sweep through the gates. There is a sense of something wrong about hiding and running – it's as if some inherent line of being a traitor has been inevitably and irretrievably crossed.

Jabu calls when all is clear. I sit up and watch the road whistle past his tiny box-car.

Northdale suburb is off a winding road that leads away from the city, jagging left moments after a right turn signposts down to a quarry and farm called 'Hope's Folly'. We swing left and I remember the news last week about a fire-fight with an ANC cell. The road right has been sealed by blue and yellow police tape, twined across the road between the trees.

Jabu opens up as we enter Indian territory, "Will your Thought Box be worth all this trouble for you, Martin?"

I am stunned, speechless.

He smiles as we drive past a cricket field, where a cricket

game is indeed going on. The teams look somewhat mixed – at least it's a motley mixture of black and brown players.

He smiles again: "A *SACOS* league Martin – *Imbali* and *Northdale* residents combined, united in calling themselves black, rather than 'Indian' or 'Bantu'."

I manage a few croaked words: "How do you know about...?"

He glances down and I see he is navigating from the cell phone secured on his dashboard. He drives his antiquated tiny Fiat hard, so that it is seemingly held together only by love and shoelaces. "I'm a good nurse, Martin, I talk to my patients. In another world, I would no doubt have been a good psychologist or psychiatrist."

"Sibusiso told you?"

Jabu turns into a close with a range of bright green and orange houses nested together, small houses, with compact gardens and seemingly sprouting from the same or a similar architectural root. He brakes to a stop, turns the engine off at the end of the close and looks at me, with a peculiar half smile on his face.

"Yes indeed he told me, Martin – can we move on quickly please?"

I realise it's been a while since he last called me 'Doctor'.

I get out of the car, wondering who else knows and whether Wadwalla would be a good lead to Sibusiso. And why was Jabu helping me track him down? He obviously knew – and had probably known for some time – that this went beyond routine hospital work. Surely his bracelet meant he had alternative loyalties too?

Jabu stands up on the other side of the car, but unlike with my larger Ford in *Imbali* last Friday, he seems to soar over his roof.

"A bit of déjà vu ne, Martin? So, do you have anything that you want to ask me?"

"Did you help him?"

He's blank for a moment and then scowls. "No! Wrong question, Martin." He slams the door and moves past me, brows furrowed, furious.

A couple are walking their baby in a pram but stop for us to step past, staring at us intently. Jabu is stalking up the small path of number 13, swinging his arms angrily. I feel alternatively ashamed and angry with myself. That is a stupid question to ask, no doubt seen as buying into the white stereotype that all black people steal. I'd just had a mad idea pop into my head that perhaps he'd been helping me all along to cover his colluding tracks – with Sibusiso – and that perhaps his 'helping' was to keep tabs on me too.

But it looks as if I was so wrong that I'd made a complete balls-up, a total *gemors* of things.

Jabu is already ringing the bell, not bothering to wait for me. I arrive at the door just as it swings open. A slight Indian woman stares out at us from behind a partly opened latched door. For a moment I don't recognize her as she's wearing slacks and a plain beige T-shirt. Then it dawns on me this is Dr. Wadwalla, who had lectured us at 'Maritzburg Varsity's PsychSoc event for OASS. Brand had snapped a photograph of her when she had been about to speak.

"Yes?" She is guarded and suspicious.

"Hello, sister," Jabu holds up his wrist.

She scans his face and then flicks her gaze to me. She has an intensely focused stare and an unsettling one at that, so I have to work hard not to break eye contact. She detaches the latch and steps aside to let us in.

The entry hall is short and opens immediately onto a small sitting area, three soft chairs and a radio/CD set in all. There is a brown wooden mantelpiece above an electric fire and some abstract art scattered across the wall, but nothing particularly Indian that I could see.

"Dr. Wadwalla." She does not offer her hand to shake, but I wonder why her head is uncovered, if she is Muslim.

"Dr. van Deventer," I say, "from Fort Napier Hospital."

"Sister Jabu Mbanga, Fort Napier Hospital."

She raises her right eyebrow but does not gesture towards the chairs, so we continue to stand awkwardly. I notice that Jabu does not look at me.

"How can I help you?" her sharp eyes suddenly seem to dull, although she keeps her body erect, alert, stiff. "Don't tell me you've been sent to certify me, have you?"

Jabu finally exchanges a glance with me. I shake my head vigorously, "I'm a psychologist not a psychiatrist, and I don't have that sort of medical authority."

"We're here about a *Fundimiso* College student who was under our care – Sibusiso Mchunu. He's in your history class, as is Nombuso, who is close to him." Jabu has leaped in.

She nods, slowly and cautiously, "I know Nombuso – but why have you come to me about them?"

"We're trying to track Sibusiso, who has disappeared," I say, trying to wrest back control of the conversation. "Nombuso is not keen to talk to us. We believe you may be able to help her open up to us, about where he is. He is not well mentally and has absconded too early from hospital. He still needs some treatment."

"Disappearances can be for good or bad reasons in this country." She turns to face me squarely, "Sister Mbanga has shown me his colours, Doctor. So how about you – where do you stand?"

How can I state my political position simply? In psychology, other psychologists have asked me how I position myself in relation to theoretical models. I straddle an eclectic, integrative position, as befits a complex and multiple-faceted reality. I have no easy position – to me that would restrain and restrict too much, opening the way to rhetoric and polarization.

"It depends," I start.

"Bullshit!"

I jump, but she has moved across to open the front door.

She steps back and gestures me out. Jabu is glaring at me again. I see the sky is darkening outside and dusk is falling. I realise then that my world is becoming increasingly fraught. There are people looking for me too; nasty people, even though they are white.

"I want everyone to have an equal stake and say in this unified country," I say, "and for us all to communicate and empathize with each other."

She closes the door. "Bravo, Doctor, that wasn't too hard, was it?"

Jabu grins at me.

She gestures to the chairs. "Sit down then, would you both like some heated *rotie* and curried mince?"

"Yes please!" Jabu and I have spoken together and we look at each other again.

I take the opportunity. "I'm – uh, sorry, Sister Mbanga," I say, "for that stupid question I asked earlier."

Jabu nods, smiles slightly and looks away, moving to sit down on a chair.

Dr. Wadwalla pauses on her way through to what smells like the kitchen in the room opposite us – although the door is only slightly ajar, aromas of cinnamon and curry seep through. "You gentlemen can call me Fariedah," she says, "And it's good to hear it sounds as if you're refining your self-awareness bullshit radar, Dr. Someone van Deventer."

"Martin," I say, feeling stung and somewhat embarrassed, "and *you* don't sound like a typical Muslim to me – if you don't mind me saying so, Fariedah."

Her head rocks back in an explosive burst of laughter that is so completely uninhibited I forget the sting of her comment. "You're a wise man indeed if you can show me a typical Muslim, Martin – although some in my family do tell me I am only a Muslim with a little 'm'."

She vanishes into the kitchen.

As for me, perhaps I am only a traitor with a small 't'?

We visit Nombuso as evening settles in, after first picking up Jacky from my dog walker, who had kept her, after I'd called her frantically earlier from my office. I have no doubt anymore that my home is being watched and is no longer safe to return to.

So Jabu swings his cramped car around the darker and lesser-travelled roads towards *Fundimiso's* residences in Imbali. Jacky licks my face and farts with excitement at the unexpected road trip. I apologise for her smells in case they think it's me and I wind the window down as the dim road speeds past us, the shacks only vague shapes in the non-electrified darkness.

Fariedah had eventually agreed with approaching Nombuso – saying we can only ask, but that we must also respect the directives within each cell. Both she and Jabu have stated that their price would be ANC membership for me. I knew of some whites who were members of course – the banned and exiled couple Ray Alexander and Jack Simons had been the first, but to me it had still felt a *huge* ask. I had seen front-page pictures of victims of bomb attacks, as well as local collaborators sitting husked and burnt, a charred tyre dropping their dead shoulders away from their blackened heads.

Of course, as they'd pointed out to me, there were no reciprocated pictures of people 'slipping' in white interrogation showers or else being shot by police or army. Censorship of the press was heavy and unilateral, Fariedah telling me that the ANC would *always* firmly oppose press censorship, should they eventually come to power.

What had finally persuaded me was the realization that I was already so deep in trouble a further step may not make *that* much difference – that, and the constantly recurring image of a sharp, smooth and deadly unmarked bullet.

Now, however, Jabu swings into the parking lot of Nombuso's college residence. Keep focused on the immediate steps in the moment, van Deventer, I tell myself as I clip on Jacky's lead.

Fariedah has also promised me residence within a safe house

of someone I knew, from where I could try and contact Dan, should I be able to get our Box back. A shadowy existence, but at least *something* – and perhaps we could get rich on it, as Dan hoped. (But we would presumably only be able to enjoy such riches should we end up leaving the land of our birth?)

Hard choices and huge moves beckon terrifyingly from the future, should I be able to stay free. Now, however, we open our doors in a quiet parking lot.

Fariedah turns to me from the front seat. "You can only take the dog if it's dead quiet."

I nod; relieved they'd allowed her in the car initially, as she was obviously not a 'racist' dog, unlike many white people's pets. Jacky's retriever genes seemed to know no race or creed.

Jabu rummages in his car's front hatch and throws a navy balaclava back at me. "Here," he says, "this is less likely to stick out than your white face."

I wonder what uses he has made of it as I pull the balaclava on. Jacky gives it the briefest of sniffs; she can always tell who I am.

"Right, let's go," says Jabu, stepping outside.

I feel like a thief as I follow Jabu and Fariedah from the parking lot towards the dorms, but no thief could ever have been seen with a wimpier dog. Jacky has taken a dislike to the new place, unsure of her bearings, perhaps afraid it's en route to the kennels. Whatever the reason, she drags behind me, tail tucked under her belly, and I have to cluck to get her to move at all.

Jabu turns to look at me and I catch his expression from a lamp post near the parking notice. I stop clucking and give Jacky firm yanks until she comes more readily, with wounded reluctance. We head towards the stairwell of the building and wind our way up three flights of the terraced block, stepping aside once for a gaggle of young girls heading down, seemingly dressed for the night and a local *jol.*

Fariedah leads the way three flats along and knocks on 3*3 (the middle number is missing). I reflect briefly that I have become aware of a wider range of living places in the past couple of days than I have experienced previously in my entire life.

The door opens and I see the sullen, shaven girl from our previous visit. She is looking drawn and tired and is about to snap a comment, before her eyes dilate as she recognizes Fariedah.

"Doctor!"

"Sorry to disturb you, Nombuso, I know it's almost eight, but we wanted to discuss something with you."

"We?" She cranes her neck out of the doorway to look Jabu and I over. "What's the *umlungu* doing here?" she asks, obviously not fooled by my balaclava.

"He's a friend," says Jabu.

"Really?" She asks, "He looks like a *boer* to me."

"Not all *boere* are the same," says Jabu, "even though most of them think *we* are."

"Oh, you're the male nurse from previously," she says, pulling her head in again. "Okay, you can come in, but the dog had better not piss or *kak* in my flat."

We step inside. Jacky and I are last in and I see it's little more than a room with a bed, one chair, table and microwave on a shelf. There are packets of instant noodles, *biltong* and *boerewors* flavoured, and a few mugs, spoons and sachets of tea and coffee.

"Sorry I can't offer you anything." Nombuso sits and winces at the edge of her bed. She is wearing stiff and plain beige pyjamas. Jabu rolls up a sleeve on his right arm.

"I saw that wound earlier," he says. "I guess you've not been able to see anyone about that?"

"It's just a scratch, a flesh wound," she says, but I see she is biting her lip.

"I am indeed a nurse," says Jabu, "with physical health training and a First Aid box in my car. Mind if I take a look?"

She stares at me sullenly, "As long as the *umlungu* turns his back."

I turn my back. Jacky strains on the lead behind me, I think to greet Nombuso, but I don't turn around to check.

Jabu grunts. "Back in a minute." I hear the door close, but stay fixed in position.

The door opens again and I see he has a first aid box under his arm.

Fariedah sits on the chair and I look at her sidelong while I wait. She is watching the procedure behind me with a straight and undaunted gaze, but flickers that gaze towards me as if aware I was looking at her. Sensitive.

She shivers and pulls a face at me as if she is watching something unpleasant. She's funny, too.

"You can turn around now, Martin," says Jabu, and I turn to see him washing his hands in a small basin in the corner of the room I'd not seen previously.

Nombuso is standing, her midriff rumpled and bulky, with a flash of white bandage still visible. Her bottom lip is bleeding but she has not made a sound.

Jabu turns to face us. "A good job, whoever did that. It looks fine – as you say, a graze, but a painful graze. It'll take a week or two to heal properly, as long as you keep it clean. I have some, but do you have more pain-killers if needed?"

Nombuso nods, as if unsure she can speak properly.

Jabu gives her tablets and a mug of water. She tosses the tablet in her mouth and swallows.

Fariedah stands up and introduces us properly, then gives me a nod to go ahead.

"I have a patient I believe you know – Sibusiso Mchunu. I have reason to believe he has made off from Fort Napier Hospital recently with something of mine."

Nombuso stares at me and says nothing. I find it disconcerting to notice that her lip still drips blood, albeit slowly.

I try again. "It's a valuable piece of equipment. I need to have it back. I would also like to see how Sibusiso is doing. Can you please tell me where he is?"

Slowly, she shakes her head. I look across at Fariedah and then Jabu, silently asking for their help.

Fariedah gives a little shrug and steps forward: "Perhaps he can ask someone above you, if you're afraid of compromising information?"

"Why should we help him?"

"He's in trouble with the authorities too," says Jabu. "He's also in the process of joining us."

Nombuso tosses her head with a slightly dismissive sneer and then stops. "Dr. van Deventer, hey?"

"Yes," I confirm, puzzled.

"I'll take you to someone then, who knows where Sibusiso is for sure," she says, "...and that's only because I remember him saying something nice about you. Although I –" (She pauses, as if for effect) "I still don't trust you."

"Oh good, thank you," I'm very relieved.

"One condition..." she holds up her right finger.

Jacky is licking Nombuso's bare left foot and she giggles, trying to keep looking stern.

"Yes?" I query, pulling Jacky back to heel.

"I'm taking you there alone on the back of my motorbike and to be sure you don't see where we're going, you're going to have to wear your balaclava back to front."

I feel weak and incredulous, "You can't be serious?"

Jabu and Fariedah are already by the door and I can see they're both trying not to smile.

Nombuso has moved over to open her wardrobe. "See you in five minutes down in the parking lot, Doctor."

We let ourselves out and head down the dimly lit stairs, which smell surprisingly of disinfectant. Someone cleans here, not all is dirt and chaos, yet another subversion of my stereotypes. I feel as if my entire world is becoming huge, but unhinged, disconnected.

We reach Jabu's car and he clicks it open. "What about Jacky?" I ask.

"I'll take her for a day or two; my kids would love that, although Mariam may not." He smiles, swinging his bulk a little on the front door and I realise how little I still really know about him. It has never really occurred to me to ask, up until now.

"Mariam is your wife?" I ask.

He nods at what must no doubt seem the obvious – but, to me, *nothing* is obvious anymore.

Fariedah stands in front of me. "A bit of advice, Martin. I've seen Nombuso on her bike. Hold on tight." Thoughtful too; then the fear kicks in.

I hand Jabu the lead. Jacky nuzzles him — she will love whoever feeds her, although she will miss me, but I have no intention of being away *too* long. "Can I call you when I'm done, about where to stay?" I ask him.

He nods. "Make sure it's from a safe line though, they have your cell number for sure. I'd toss your cell if I were you."

I'm a novice, completely out of my depth at this.

I grind the phone under my heel.

Just then, I hear the stifled roar of a motorbike and a black-clad rider emerges from what must have been a secure bike shed, off from a corner of the parking lot. There's a screech of tyres, a burning smell, smoke and the rider soars through to us on her back wheel, having pulled an outrageous wheelie.

My legs start to shake.

Jacky barks, freaked out by the display and I see a group of students around a nearby car turn to stare at us.

Nombuso drops her front wheel as she pulls up alongside us and holds another helmet out towards me. "When I shout 'right', you lean right. Same goes for left. Always lean the way I do, never the opposite. And, Doctor..."

I have taken the balaclava off, ready to turn it around. I look up at her visored face, too frightened to speak.

"Don't touch me, okay? My ribs are hell – so hold onto the struts at the back of the bike here," she indicates a small bar. "Touch me with your hands and I drop you off *wherever* we are. You find your own way home then, on foot – and it's not a sweet white suburb we'll be traveling through right now."

I nod stiffly, hoping she will change her mind about the balaclava.

It's hard to see her eyes behind the visor and in the dim light, but I have no doubt they do not waver. "Put it on then, but back to front, mind you."

I see that the students from the nearby car are walking our way. I glance, panic-stricken at Fariedah. She's watching me. Yes, and beautiful too.

Ag, come off it, van Deventer, there is no possible future together; it's well known that SB agents wait outside bedroom doors, ready to strip bed sheets for Immorality Act evidence while licking their lips for a climax through keyholes.

Just put the fucking helmet on, you're kak with women anyway – that, at least, is a given!

I can see nothing with navy blue wool in my eyes. Jabu, I think, takes the helmet from me and places it on my head, strapping it under my chin.

I hear Nombuso talking with the students in Zulu, but have no idea what they are saying. The world is both dark and scary.

Jabu lifts me under the arm and swings my leg onto the back of the pillion. Nombuso's warmth is in front of me, but she shuffles forward a bit. Jabu helps me place my hands on the back strut.

I brace myself.

The bike growls and I can feel the rising power surging beneath me. I can only clamp my thighs as if I were riding a horse. She pops the clutch and the bike bucks and surges forward, my neck snaps back and I am only saved from falling off by the terrified rigidity in my braced arms.

I do not touch her, but I am glad she has moved forward.

I am wetting myself.

I cannot quite believe it, but we've finally come to a standstill.

Sobbing softly through stuffy wool, I place my feet down on either side, feeling the safety of a firm surface. My arms have frozen into place behind me and I can't seem to remember how to open my hands. My shoulders ache deep across my back, but I'm mostly aware of my wet crotch. Please, God, may it not show through into my beige *Chinos*.

I hear voices and someone is alongside and massaging my arms, finally pulling my fingers off the bar behind me, one by one. Then they manoeuvre my left leg over the back of the bike and have to hold me up, my legs are shaking so much.

"*Hayi*, Nombuso," I hear an admonishing voice, a female voice, but of a deep and gruff tone, "You've frightened this one so much he's wet himself!"

Oh, shit.

Nombuso laughs and there's a rapid exchange of Zulu, before I am led forward by the right arm and shoulder: "Mind the steps." The second voice, although gruff, is perhaps kinder than Nombuso's – whom I would have *loved* to certify, if I'd been a psychiatrist.

A knock and the creaking sound of a door opening. Even though my nose is covered by the tickly wool – and boy, how that balaclava tickled my nose the whole fucking journey – I smell a mixed scent of foods, both meat and vegetable.

"You can take off the helmet." There's a new woman's voice, this one is strong, mature, commanding.

The woman next to me tries to undo the strap but I knock her hand away and start unbuckling it myself, despite my clumsy, chilled fingers. I need to take charge of this as much as I can, standing cross-legged to minimize any further views of the wet patch at the front of my trousers.

I drop the helmet rebelliously and tear off the balaclava.

A large woman stands cross-armed, anchored in her size and authority. At first I feel less fat and then I feel less secure, for she appears comfortable in her own body.

The room is well lit by a scattering of kerosene lamps.

"Sally Jones," she says, offering me her hand, a slight smile creasing her lips.

"*Ja* right," I say, ignoring her hand, "I believe you have something of mine."

Her ghost of a smile materialises further, into a grin: "You are a direct man indeed, Doctor."

I glance around me. It's a basic home, one entrance room geared for sitting, three others apparently branching off, front and sides. I doubt it's much bigger than the four rooms at most. There are pictures of 'Sally' and a man on the wall, sometimes alone, a few with a biggish group of children. The most recent looking photo across the room on the door to the right is of 'Sally', who is on her own. It's a more solemn picture than the others, almost sad.

Nombuso is slouching down on one of the chairs, helmet hanging from her right hand, legs draped out in front of her, one boot on another chair. Having delivered me here, she now looks bored.

A woman steps past me, medium height, medium build and with neat medium length, corn-row plaits. There's nothing medium or moderate about the kick she gives Nombuso's offending foot, though. It swings off the chair and she's up in a flash, snarling. They're squaring up to each other, but the large woman – so-called Sally – is looking angry.

"Tcchhhaahhh!" She shouts, short and sharp. "Stop. You will wake my boy. Nombuso, show a little more respect for our guest, white though he is. Mandisa, wait for my word before you act on anything and everything, okay?"

"Sorry, *Mamma*," says Mandisa, and I smile at 'Sally's' brief flash of further irritation. Still, lots of women are called 'mother'.

Nombuso goes to sit at the furthest chair but keeps a watchful eye on me. Mandisa refuses to sit, but leaves the house, muttering she will be outside for a smoke.

"Would you like a drink, Doctor – something hot – or cold – perhaps?"

"My Box," I say, "That's all I've come for."

She shakes her head and looks at me with a levelled and

discomfiting gaze for some moments. "Tell me, Doctor, when you met with Sibusiso, what did you see?"

"A depressed young man," I say. "Perhaps with some PTSD, after suffering trauma at a protest march."

She smiles and makes her way to the chair Nombuso had sprung from, sitting down gracefully: "Some of your kind now call it CTSD I believe – Continuous Traumatic Stress Disorder – given we are stressed all the time, by this illegitimate state."

I feel uncomfortable and a little rude, standing up and looking down on her, "Yes, I've heard the term amongst some of the OASS psychologists."

"But it takes you some time before you shift *your* words, perhaps?"

I sit opposite her. The woman intrigues me. "I'm cautious by nature, yes."

She seems to spill over the chair with her body, yet is self-contained. Her brown eyes are somehow both warm *and* hard. When she leans forward, her words gain extra punching power. "Ah, but whose nature are we talking about here, Doctor? What is truly 'yours' – and what comes from all who have been before you, or indeed, what has been around you? You carry some demanding confidence here too, in *my* home, a white power confidence, despite the patch on your trousers."

To my left Nombuso laughs, a short, sharp bark.

I do not break eye contact with my host.

"Smooth and clever words... oh woman who is scared to tell me her real name."

Nombuso smiles, "And what do you think your name is, Doctor? Is it 'Doctor', which you wield like a weapon before you, is it a thoughtful or even an arbitrary label your parents drop onto you – or is it what *you* wish to call yourself?"

"Yes, I'll have some tea, please," I hold my hand out, "My name is Martin; Martin van Deventer."

She shakes my hand, firmly, powerfully. "Good to meet you Martin. I'm Sally – Sally Jones."

Ja right, I think, but her grip is fleshy and firm, *whatever* her name is.

It hits me then. Here, my knowledge counts for little.

The more I've chased Sibusiso and my box, the less certain I've become.

Of anything.

Words do not come; I feel psychological models crack inside my head.

"Martin?" Mamma has stood up in front of me, solicitous in attitude, revealing what looks like genuine concern.

I smile at the irony; the state of my trousers is an irrelevance.

I stand, bow and kiss her hand.

She does not pull away.

When I leave, after a hot cup of rooibos tea, she gives me a cell, a mobile phone only for 'emergency' text use.

"Just in case," she says.

I pocket the phone reluctantly, hoping never to feel it buzz or hear it ring.

Chapter 13
Sibusiso Comes Home

The trip home is shorter. From Maputo, we have a large speedboat, manned by two serious Chinese men with expensive looking clothes and phones, dark glasses and no conversation – at least not for us.

The taller one with a shaving shadow on his lip knows how to handle the boat, though. The shorter one watches his phone and barks orders, with the boat careering and swerving at a rapid speed, bouncing over the swell. I think it has a radar app linked to a military intelligence centre, but perhaps that's just my fantasy.

At least this time I am not sick. There is not the slightest hint of a fishy smell on board. The only smell is the petrol we burn from the twin 120hp engines. I am propped between Xolile and Numbers where we sit at the back, being caught by the occasional spray from the bucking boat.

We sit and say little ourselves, because we are changed men.

It was the rail journey from Lusaka to Maputo that did it. We had time to kill and so we played with the EmPods the Chinese gave us in return. Small portable mind-reading devices that fit in the palm of your hand, with tiny clips and scalp nets that just cover Broca's area, apparently. ('Em' stands for Empathy and also 'M' for Mind.)

But empathy comes from within – sometimes it may be better *not* knowing what is inside another person. Our words eventually slowed, as we grew to know each other more – and perhaps a little more than what we felt was comfortable.

Even now, as I see a white strip of beach sand come into focus, a South African beach – home, but not fully *ours*, we stay quiet, saying nothing.

We each have backpack bags with a hundred EmPods in them – and that's just the start. We gather others will be equipped to bring these small machines into South Africa too. They have been rigged so that you get scores for how many people you empathize with – you plug in demographic details through a wireless keyboard and it gives you even more points for empathizing with someone from another so-called race or culture. There are also additional points for empathizing with a different gender, more for the greater the age difference etcetera, etcetera. Empathy is measured by how accurately you think back the image or words you have received; the machine detects and calibrates the accuracies of these reflected brain patterns.

The Chinese have turned the doctor's mind-reading machine into an addictive video game, but without the video. "It will make a killer app, too," said Chung Li when we left, but he failed to give us further details on this. Knowing the Chinese just a little bit, it may already be waiting for us as we arrive back in South Africa, hanging in the illicit cyber-clouds that the government fails to fully deseed.

As for the EmPod beta version, it just has an accumulative points read out with no other pay off. But it seems points alone can be utterly addictive. Chung Li has told us the follow-up version may contain a neurally invoked emotional payload, to deepen available game rewards.

As for us, we played each other until it got too scary.

Numbers is full of numbers; to help hide the blood he has seen or spilled, I think. I never managed to get a clear glimpse, the blood hovered on the edge of things, smearing all his thoughts – it appeared to be wilfully covered by his constant calculations. Xolile is torn between word-visions of his friends in Zambia and his home near Port St. John, where his family still lives. The sadness for his split life hangs heavily on me. What I did increasingly better with, however, was decoding Xolile's thoughts on cricket.

The taller Chinese man is winding the boat's speed down as the shorter man scours the beach with a pair of binoculars. The palms are draping down towards the beach, which looks both beautiful and deserted.

The other two haven't told me what they've made of *my* thoughts. As the games fizzled out when we approached Maputo, so too did our conversations. Xolile won by a huge margin, but at least I didn't come last.

Numbers cracks his knuckles with a sound that makes me think of a cracking neck.

The boat has drifted to a standstill, just a few metres short of the empty beach.

The shorter man talks: "It is good to walk from here, only a small bit of you will get wet. Car is on other side of trees."

I am not tempted to try EmPodding either man with our Empathy game, no matter how many points I may accrue.

We remove our donated sandals and step out of the boat into warm, knee-deep water and wet sand, which sinks slightly underfoot. Numbers leads the trudge ashore.

Home soil, land of our birth, where we have yet to claim our full and due citizenship rights.

The boat roars off and a wave laps at my heels. No one has bothered to say goodbye to anyone.

A woman appears through the dense leaves at the head of the beach. She is large, with a mane of black hair that sprouts from her, as if she were a male lion. There is nothing male about the generous curves of the rest of her body, though, her rainbow blouse is attractively stretched, her wide hips wrapped in a bright red *kikoi*.

I know who she is straight away, as do the others, I'm sure.

It's Numbers she greets first, though.

He kisses her hand, "Mamma!"

She smiles at us, "You must all be tired, it's been a long journey for you all – and within the space of little less than a week, too."

Xolile and I nod, but Numbers remains impassive, as if he doesn't know what she is talking about. She chuckles and asks, "You have the Box and the Chinese copies, then?"

Numbers taps the bag on his back with his right hand.

"Good, come," she says, turning to push her way through the leaves.

Numbers muscles himself around and ahead of her, in order to untangle the narrow, covered path. Both Xolile and I put our sandals on, but Numbers has not bothered. He has secured them on top of his swinging backpack.

His bulk bursts through the last of the foliage and we see a small and battered minibus vehicle parked on the verge of a gravel circle. A wiry woman leans against the side of the passenger seat, smoking. She drops the cigarette and stamps it out as we emerge from the strip of *strandveld* forest, making her way around to the driver's door, clicking it open.

"A typical taxi," says Mamma, "We will attract a *lot* less attention that way, than if we had secured one of those large government Mercs to travel in. *When* we get into power, I am sure we will keep our vehicles small and light on the planet. We will not be seduced by excess or money."

All three of us look at her. She had said 'when' and not 'if'.

The driver opens the door for her, by leaning across the gears and handbrake. Mamma slides in with apparent ease, muscles working well, despite her bulk. "I'm sure you boys don't mind sitting at the back."

I am the meat in the middle of the human sandwich on the long seat. We sit as if expecting more passengers. The driver grunts and engages her gears, skidding slightly on the dusty gravel for several minutes before grinding to a halt. She jumps from the front and strides towards some tape tied between two trees. It's blue and yellow police 'do not cross' tape. She cuts the tape free and spools it into her pocket.

"We got that from a useful contact," says Mamma, "and it was one way to try and ensure our privacy here."

"You said 'when' we are in power, Mamma," says Xolile. "Has anything changed while we have been away?"

Mamma swivels to look at us. She is not so filled with her

own importance that she would speak to the air in front of her. "Things always change. This time, though, they are changing faster. Obama is now putting pressure on the apartheid government – and with Russian peace talks, the old anti-communist arguments for supporting this government are falling. Sanctions have already weakened the will of many of the white people here."

"It's a matter of time," says the driver, in a rough tone, swinging carefully onto the large tarred road.

"*Yebo*, Mandisa, it is indeed just time and..." Mamma turns again and fixes me with her gaze. "The white government now feels like a fragile pack of cards stacked up, ready to collapse – and your doctor's box may be one of the flicking fingers that helps to topple the lot."

"Really, Mamma," I ask, "How?"

"I'll tell you soon enough," she says. "*He* came looking for his Box too, you know, the night before last. Nombuso brought him to my house..."

This stuns me, but Mandisa is swearing as the traffic is particularly heavy and slowing us down. She ignores four young men with football shirts, as well as an old woman signing at us from the side of the road, wanting a trip in to town. Instead, she grinds her gears angrily.

Mamma shoots her a reproving look: "Calm down girl, we won't miss the collapse of this government if you drive a little more slowly."

Mandisa just grates her teeth and hoots at the car ahead of us. "I've got to look like a *real* taxi, Mamma!"

We laugh – even Numbers chuckles.

"Sobukwe may be an old man, Mamma," he says, "But he told me in Kitwe that the PAC wants to rename the country."

Mamma grunts and turns to me, but a little less easily and I see strain lines on her face. It seems that she too is feeling the pinch of a journey. "I'll tell you soon enough, Sibusiso," she says, "But first, we've got to do a deal with some low-lifes."

"Fuck!" Mandisa's face is thrust forward, staring hard through her windscreen. It is no wonder the traffic is slow. We are approaching the Lower Umgeni River Bridge and a police vehicle is parked facing us by the side of the road leading onto the bridge.

A cop is waving us off for inspection. He's small for a *boere*, clean shaven and wearing a cap that looks too big for his prickly scalp. His partner, a larger and darker looking man, perhaps a 'coloured', is making notes into his cell, leaning against his passenger door. He flashes his cell at us, as if taking a picture.

"Take it easy, Mandisa, perhaps they just want to ask a few questions." Mamma is focused forward now, but her voice remains cool and even. She winds down her window, as does Mandisa, slowly slipping the *kombi* off the road, rolling it to a halt in front of the cop car. The traffic begins to roll past as the white cop saunters over to Mandisa's window.

He swings his blue eyed gaze across us all and I feel Numbers tense to my left, although we have carried no weapons from the boat.

The cop turns his gaze to Mandisa: "Trrravelling a little light, aren't we, considering the big soccer game today?"

She shrugs. "I don't pick up football fans who look like *tsotsis*."

'Hmm...." he looks across to Mamma."Howzzz about you all step outside, so we can check your vehicle."

The bang hurts my ears. The cop looks surprised and staggers back a few steps, his cap falling off. Then I see blood spurting down his face, from a hole above his right eye.

There is a bang from the side of the road and the window shatters to my left. I scramble down, into the open bench space in front of me. Then there is a rattling series of bangs from the front seat and, suddenly, a painful silence.

Mamma's voice drifts over my head from the front seat. "Both cops are down. Drive like hell, Mandisa."

The *kombi* revs up and with a sudden roar, it swerves

forward onto the bridge, pushing me back against the seat I'd left. A heavy weight tumbles onto my back and head and I fall forward again, face grinding against the floor.

There's another loud bang from the front seat. "No one follows," says Mamma, "and they pull over ahead of us. My AK has warned them."

"Mamma..." it sounds like Xolile's voice, although also not quite like him.

"Yes!" she snaps as we swerve again: "Get off this road the other side of the bridge as soon as you can, Mandisa, I'll rig the satnav to take us up the back routes."

"Mamma..." calls Xolile again, in his weird almost not-him voice.

I can't sit up, the weight is too heavy, crushing me, and something is trickling down my neck. Oh shit, have I been shot? Has my body gone dead and heavy on me, because I've been shot?

"Mamma, Numbers is dead." It is Xolile's voice. A large hand and arm with tattooed numbers flops down near my face. I realise there is a body on my back. A *big* body.

I scream.

I never knew Numbers had a family.

For those few hours we had mind-read each other, I had not glimpsed that at all. In our terse conversations, there had been no hint of any others he may have cared for.

And certainly not this large weeping woman, with two small children tugging at the hem of her dress. We stand bowed around his body, laid out on a bed in a small house, creaking with a cheap and temporary aluminium room extension. Some neighbours have come in too, gaping behind us.

Mamma raises her hands: "For the spirit of Numbers. May he rest in peace and not need to lurk anywhere nearby. May the *amadlozi* guide him in good company."

The woman sobs even louder, one child clutches her

mother's dress tighter and the other drops like a small stone onto the dead man, her face streaked with silent tears.

"I have called a doctor sympathetic to our cause, Mamma," says Mandisa, moving alongside her.

Mamma nods, muttering so that only the closest can hear, "And for the families of those other two men." She turns to leave, the gathering crowd behind her spilling out and before her by the door and outside, onto the street.

"Those cops who killed him?" hissed Mandisa at her shoulder.

"Have families too," says Mamma shortly. She bows respectfully at a nondescript old man approaching the house, "My greetings, sir."

He nods at her, but stiffly: "More dead in your wake, Nqobile?"

She stiffens slightly, "For a future in which only the old and ill need fear death."

He laughs, "Like me, perhaps?"

She bows and turns, as if empty of words. I catch a glimpse of her face – her cheeks are wet too.

Four of us climb into a small battered car and sit silently for moments.

"Not all agree with our methods, even here," says Mamma.

But there is no need to say anything.

I am sitting at the back again and stare out of the window at smoke rising behind the trees. The *kombi* had burst into flames immediately when Xolile threw the match, after it had been doused in petrol. But it smokes as if burning still, more than an hour in, as if finding the blood on its seats hard to digest.

9-1-1 were the most recurring numbers I'd seen in Numbers' head – the emergency call for help.

Mamma sighs. "Let's go and meet those *tsotsis*, Mandisa. I feel like leaning heavily on some people who deserve it."

My body still feels heavy, as if a larger body sprawls upon it. Inside me, though, I feel the Beast stirring again, growling softly as it wakes.

She is growing even more in strength, so I must handle her both well and with care. She?

And why do I also catch a glimpse in my mind of a ghostly bird I saw at Hope's Folly, flashing across my vision with its funny wedged shaped bill?

It is a big house in what looks like the better part of *Imbali* township. The walls are new, fresh and lean well, smacking of money. Lots of money. There's even a swimming pool in the back garden, I spot it from a window as we climb the stairs to meet the boss-man on the next floor. This house is a *double story, nogal!*

Ahead and behind us walks a man with a cocked gun, but no one else seems afraid. Mamma leads our group up the stairs with a quiet assuredness and silent steps. Mandisa brings up the rear for us – we men are in the middle, lacking weapons I guess, although Xolile is humming to himself. He has his cell radio plugged into his left ear, listening to a cricket commentary of Australia v India.

The room at the top is plush, carpeted and furnished with soft leather couches of different colours – four wide ones, pink, purple, green and yellow. The carpet itself is a mélange of abstract colours and swirls that makes me feel giddy for a moment.

We stop, but it takes me a further moment to spot the small man fixing himself a drink at a bar counter on the far side of the room. I hear the clink of ice on glass but all I see is the back of a sharp grey suit and shiny black Italian looking shoes.

The man turns to face us with a glass of whisky perhaps, swirling like liquid gold in his crystal glass. He has a narrow face and an even thinner smile, underlined by a forked goatee beard.

"Hey man," he speaks English, "How are you dudes hanging?"

His speech is strange, affected, but I know better than to laugh. His two bodyguards have fanned out to the other corners of the room, guns still alert.

Mamma spreads her feet, as if straddling this new space with her authority. She has long removed her bright *kikoi*. Underneath this, her camouflaged military style trousers carry a sterner but silent message. Her strapped boots match well, but she still wears her rainbow blouse - and wears it proudly. She replies in *isiZulu*.

"Another one has died for change, Tsepo..."

"You must change your business, Mamma – mine is safer, as I've always said, why not join me?"

She smiles, but it's a fleeting flash; this is all clearly part of an older dance of words between them.

"Numbers is gone," she says shortly. I see she must have dried her face before entering the building.

Tsepo startles and the glass clinks in his hand. He takes a quick sip. "I thought that big bastard was built to last forever."

"None of us are." She gestures at us and all three of us remove the bags from our backs.

The two men at the corners of the room level their guns, but Tsepo waves them down. "What's your merchandise?" he asks.

"Three hundred units, to be delivered as free sweeteners with your drug route into the white areas."

"Free?" Tsepo looks incredulous: "Since when has anything been free?"

Mamma takes a small brown box out of Mandisa's bag and tosses it to Tsepo. He catches it neatly with one hand. Xolile gives him a short clap, but then I notice his ear pod is still inserted, so perhaps the clap is not for Tsepo, but for an Indian batsman or bowler.

He puts his glass down on the copper table and thumbs the box open, pulling the slim EmPod out. "What is it? It doesn't look like it can be smoked or snorted."

"An involuntary gift from a white doctor – and a voluntary gift from the Chinese government. It's a game that will help dissolve apartheid barriers. We have runners bringing lots more in, as we speak. We need you to spread them as widely as you can, amongst your white clientele."

He throws it high in the air and catches it. Xolile claps again and I notice that he has taken his ear pod out.

"Payment for our services?"

"We don't shut you down right now."

He hisses; taking a step forward and the men at the two corners of the room level their guns. "You're not the police; you have no authority here."

"No, we're not the police – *yet*, Tsepo. Do you really want to cross MK?"

They level their gazes at each other. Tsepo is the first to look down. He steps back and tosses the light box in his hand thoughtfully, "Our rates for *dagga* have dropped, even for the best of our *Durban Poison*, perhaps these boxes will help add to our prices."

"It's been hard times for us all – and I said 'free', Tsepo."

He tosses the box onto the yellow couch. "Sure, Mamma, I heard you the first time. Okey-dokey, my groovy cats, do you fancy a drink on Uncle Tsepo?"

This time Mamma does reply in English, as she turns and gestures at us to leave. "No."

Chapter 14
Martin's Fight

Doctor Ronald James' house is not what I expected.

For a start, it's larger, with two extra bedrooms that have been painted over, whited out, an underlying hint of blue in one, pink in the other. Mrs. Gertie James – slightly bent but still sprightly, offers me the vaguely pink room.

"It used to be Michelle's," she says, "But she's away in res at Wits, doing medicine."

Although her eyes are lively and dance in her face as she talks, there is a hint of sadness that discourages me asking about the ex-blue room.

Dr. James – uh, *Ronald* – has remained behind in the lounge. I can tell from the stink of smoke as we pass the lounge door, so that she can show me where the toilet is, that he is now deep into his pipe.

It was late and I had been half-stunned when the door opened, revealing him standing there in his night-gown after Mandisa had knocked. He, too, had looked surprised, but he had recovered quickly and told Mandisa that he was happy to cover me for a week at most – but "more if Mamma really needs it." 'Sally' is 'Mamma' too, no doubt – but I wonder who she truly mothers.

We return to the lounge and... Ronald stands there, pipe in hand, looking at a picture on the mantelpiece. Three young people; a long-haired girl in the middle, between an older boy with a scraggly moustache trying to assert his maturity on her left, in starched brown army uniform, a much younger boy in striped school uniform on her right.

I step hesitantly into the room, restraining a cough.

Ronald half turns and taps his pipe into an ashtray on his mantelpiece. The ash still glows. He knocks the framed photo with the mouthpiece of his pipe.

"You're the first person we've had to stay here, since they've... gone, Martin."

I don't know what to say to that, so I say nothing.

He points with the mouthpiece of his pipe at a chair, so I sit, wondering at how effectively the pipe seems to extend his personhood.

He sits too, opposite me; "You've hidden your political viewpoints well, Martin."

I *have* to laugh then. And laugh, and laugh again.

He places his pipe down on an ashtray on the wooden coffee table between us – the ashtray is solid, round, grey metal, unadorned. Leaning back, he clasps his hands in front of his red dragon illustrated Chinese looking silk robe and waits for me.

It's Gertie coming in with a tray of mugs, teapot and Lemon Creams that settles my stomach and heart, stopping my laughter. I glance at the clock above the mantelpiece. It's after midnight.

"Sorry," I say. "You hide your views well too, Ronald, although I always wondered about your green *takkies*."

He smiles and then looks up to thank his wife as she gives him a mug. "We English are used to hiding things," he says, stirring his mug. "You gave me a right ticking off last time we spoke, I recall."

My face heats up as I take the mug of Earl Grey and thank Gertie, who nods briefly in acknowledgement. "I'm very sorry," I say. "I thought you'd sold me out to the Special Branch about my EE Box."

"So I gather," he says, taking a cautious sip, "but 'twas not I."

"Then who?" Out of the corner of my eye, Gertie takes a seat too with her mug, the tray of biscuits between us all. I reach out and take two, sandwiching them together, so that it looks like one.

He shrugs. "The boy you tried it on has no doubt told others. The hospital itself is a hothouse of ears for all sorts of views; I sometimes think madness itself is just a distraction from the sweeping psychosis that has gripped our country for decades."

"What happened?" I ask.

"Eh –?" he looks at me blankly.

But Gertie understands.

She puts her mug down and I dunk my biscuits.

"John was killed when in the army in Namibia," she says, "And George is in England, having been smuggled out by Mamma when he got too excited with student politics in Durban."

Ronald has put his mug down too and sweeps his arms expansively: "Two brothers raised together with radically different political beliefs from within the same family. Explain that to me, in terms of nature and nurture, Martin."

I can explain little, so I continue to chew guiltily on the soggy but tangy biscuits in my mouth.

Gertie places mugs back on the tray: "Do you have any longer term plans? You do know of course that you have to lie low while you're here and not contact anyone."

My mouth is empty again, so I can talk, even though it feels I have little to say. "Sally – I mean, *Mamma*, has promised me my EE Box will be returned to me by Sibusiso."

Ronald looks puzzled, so I fill him in as sketchily as I can manage. "The patient I practised the Box on ended up stealing it, seemingly for the ANC."

"Why?" Ronald is fiddling with his pipe again, as if itching to light it.

"No idea," I say. "She wouldn't tell me much. As for me, I'll lie low for a while, as you say, perhaps until it all dies down and they forget about me."

Ronald laughs and I realise it is the first time I have ever seen him laugh. He laughs with a wide mouth, rocking back, suddenly strangely open, almost vulnerable. He recovers himself quickly though: "That's the point I'm afraid, Martin, this government never forgets – particularly with what we the English did to their women and children in the Boer War. Everything since then has been about making sure that never happens to them again."

Exhausted, I stand up, "Then the only thing I can think of right now is to go to bed. Thank you both again for your generous and brave hospitality."

I leave them, Ronald lighting up, Gertie looking across to the photograph of her children on the mantelpiece.

The faux white room has a comfortable bed, but I lie awake after a fraught and never-ending day, feeling I have been hosted in just about every type of accommodation in 'Maritzburg.

Yet, despite all of this, I have a sense of being completely and utterly *kapoet* and *klaar*.

Despite my exhaustion, I have not even had a firm glimpse of my EE Box. Do promises even count anymore in today's cutthroat world, especially in South Africa?

It's a nice bed, but it's not mine.

I wonder if the Jameses would mind having Jacky join us.

After 2:15 am, I stop looking at the bedside clock.

I manage to stay quiet for the better part of three days and even cook up a meal for my hosts the first night, defrosting a frozen chicken and grilling it with garlic flakes, microwaving some frozen assorted veg. By lunchtime of day three I'm missing work, my laptop and the Internet. Ronald had decoupled our I-net access; just in case any spybots track my activity on their computer – it's been frustrating days since I last updated my Arse-Book account.

Gertie works too and had said I could borrow her car if I needed to, as long as I kept away from any old haunts – including home – and wore a hat and a pair of non-prescription dark glasses they offered me, but I don't want to drive around looking like a complete *doos*. They'd warned me away from Jabu, in case he was being watched, so I couldn't even visit Jacky. (It seems that *both* of the Jameses are allergic to dogs – tragic!)

I chew a cheese and tomato sandwich over my eighty ninth game of Solitaire on their laptop. I need a plan, a strategy, something to carry me forward with at least a modicum of hope in the days ahead. It's hot as hell, so I sit on the veranda wearing one of Ronald's few but tight T-shirts, which I stretch to its limit, looking towards the road as the traffic dribbles past.

I spot a pizza boy on a learner's scooter driving past – but he slows…and is coming in? Then I realise there is no pizza label on the box at the back of his bike; on the front is a small satnav. I snap the laptop screen shut, heart racing, as the driver breaks unsteadily on the driveway in front of me. He unclips his helmet and I see Sibusiso grinning in front of me.

"You bastard," I say, stepping off the veranda, "Where have you been and where's my EE Box?"

He glances around warily and places a finger in front of his lips. Stepping off the scooter, he opens the wooden pizza-basket on the back and lifts out my Box, having dropped his helmet in order to manage this. He carries it over to me carefully and offers it to me, tongue sticking out of the side of his mouth in concentration. "Here it is, Doctor, I was asked to steal, er, borrow it for the good of the country."

I cup the Box in between my hands, turning it around slowly. It looks exactly as it did, although with a few scratch marks and specks of sand. I also catch a faint whiff of fish.

"I think we should step onto the *stoep* to get away from any prying eyes, Doctor," he says, picking his helmet up.

I retreat back onto the veranda, obscured from the street and place the Box gently down onto the table. "*Where* have you been, Sibusiso?"

He shrugs awkwardly, "Out of the country."

"Really?" I'm agog, "Where?"

He shrugs again, "It's a long story and there's no time to tell it right now. I have to go. I'm sorry I stole from you."

I look at him and wonder if he's grown in the week plus

since I last saw him. His shoulders look a trifle squarer too, as if he's become more solid.

"We didn't finish our sessions," I say. It would be good to talk with him again.

He puts his helmet back on and fastens the clip under his chin. "I've finished with it all, thank you, Doctor. I will call my father soon; although I believe my family have had to move, because of what I've been doing lately, just in case."

"I know how that feels," I say. "So do you feel cured then?"

He laughs, a throaty chuckle and a flash of life from the old Sibusiso. "What's 'cured' then, Doctor? Please tell me."

"You know, no longer depressed. Happy."

"Only the mad or the privileged can be happy in this country right now."

"Oh." I think. "Well, do you feel a little less sad, then?"

He smiles, "Yes – and thank you again, Doctor. I've also come to know that I carry a Beast and a Bird within me."

Oh, shit! "Are you serious, Sibusiso? That could mean we need to get you back to the hospital."

"No!" He shouts; all smiles or hint of a smile gone from his face. He steps forward and pokes a forceful finger into my chest, almost toppling me over. "You carry a beast within you too, even if you don't know it! Stop – squeezing – my – world – into – yours." (He punctuates each word of his last sentence with a vigorous poke, so that on the last word, I collapse back into my chair.)

"The Beast is mine," he says, readying his helmet. "The Bird I've yet to recognise."

And then he is down the stairs, gently revving his bike, before turning out of the drive without turning to look back.

I know what to do now.

Carefully I pack the EE box in a cushioned bag in Gertie's Vauxhall boot and drive slowly down to the local shopping area. I am a cautious man now, wearing a floppy cricket hat advertising the Natal Dolphins and a square set of dark glasses. I park nearby what must be one of the last pay-phones in the area. Digging out some change, I give Dan's office a call.

It rings four times and I'm about to give up when a familiar voice crackles down the line: "Doctor Botha here."

"Dan?"

Silence.

"Dan?"

"Where – the – fuck – have – you – been?"

I'm grateful I'm well away from his fingers – and his fists. "Things have become – er, complicated."

"Do you still have the Box?"

"Yes, and I'm fine thank you, how about you?" I'm irked.

"Sorry," he says. "Things haven't been easy on my side either; the fucking SB have been watching our house. I think they suspect something."

"Oh God," I say. "Brand still gives me the creeps."

"Listen, we're going to have to meet somewhere neutral, somewhere safe. You remember the Pine Nut Motel?"

My heart sinks. Perhaps it will be better in the daylight. "Ja."

"See you there in half an hour. Make sure you're not tailed."

"You too," I say. *Click*! He hasn't even bothered to say goodbye.

I make my way back to the car, swinging my gaze warily around, but the place is quiet, most good white folk being at work or school. I don't need Gertie's satnav for this trip. I'm there in twenty minutes flat.

The parking lot looks even messier than it did last week at night. Scraps of newspapers flutter around, as the wind whisks itself up for the late afternoon storm. I leave the hat and glasses in the car's cubby hole and kick a couple of spent condoms out of the way as I head for the reception. The building squats low, as if ashamed of itself. The lobby area is deserted, not even a security guard in sight.

I know now to make my way to the reception desk, where

the same swarthy man from the other night watches a large split screen, his back turned to me. Eight split shots are in view and I suddenly realise they are room CCTV shots, all with various sexual activities happening in them. The receptionist has his left hand inside his trousers.

He hears my shoes squeak and hits the screen-saver button, swivelling around with both hands in view. I avoid looking too closely at his left hand.

"I'm here to see Mr. Smit in Room 129 again."

He opens his mouth, but I don't give him a chance. "And yes, I *still* like men – but if you take the slightest peek into that room, I'll have privacy lawyers abseiling off your fucking roof, you get me?"

He shuts his mouth and nods. (Sometimes a hint of money and law is more frightening than a gun. Besides, I'd had a good look at his screen. I'm betting he has some homo action in his venue, but he'd only chosen to watch hetero.)

I find my way to room 129 and knock, but there is no answer. I guess I'm a few minutes early. I try the door and it's unlocked.

I step inside, slinging the bag off my back and placing it on the floor. I'd spotted the angle of the CCTV cameras; kicking off my shoes, I step onto the sagging bed, stretching and poking at the light-fitting join at the ceiling with a pen. There's a fold of plaster, which falls away to reveal ceiling board. I poke my way around the entire fold, destroying the decoration.

It is indeed more than decoration. There's a small glass camera in a plastic chip under the last pieces of plaster, which I prise loose with the pen. I manage to catch it with my left hand before it falls. Stepping off the bed, I put my shoes back on. I place the camera on the floor and feel it 'crack' under my right heel. With my weight, there's no way he'll get *that* working again.

The door opens and Dan looks at me with bemusement, "What on Earth are you doing?"

"Destroying a camera," I say, "Jesus, you look *kak*."

He's drawn and pale, "You don't look like a pinup yourself, *boet*!"

He spots the EE Box and is across the room in a flash, picking it up and stroking it possessively. "Where the hell have you been, Martin? I've phoned; e-mailed and left zillions of messages."

"The SB are after me," I say. "I've had to be on the move and lie low."

"They want this Box badly," he says, stroking it again, in an almost pervy kind of way.

I bend to pick up pieces of glass and plastic, to throw them in the bin. "Ja, I guess it'll make their interrogations a lot easier."

"And what the fuck did you say to Helen?"

"Eh –?" I look at him blankly, "Nothing. Why?"

"She's kicked me out." He scowls, cradling the Box under his left armpit. "Did you tell her I've been seeing other women?"

"No, I haven't had a word, nor seen her, since that evening at your house." I'm standing still now, paying him my full attention, he seems strangely jittery and out of sorts.

"And how come I'm fighting a patent application with the fucking Chinese government on this Box?"

"What?" He's lost me completely.

"I thought they were supposed to be *communists*, for Christ's Sake. How the fuck can they pursue a Western Intellectual Property ownership license?"

"Dan, I've got no idea..."

He cups his chin with his right hand, index finger slanting up alongside his nose, as he used to do many years ago at school, when his temper would snap. He points his left index finger at me. (Oh, how I am tired of pointing fingers!) "Still, I'm taking charge of this now – as of today, this is my fucking machine and mine alone."

I'm cold now, despite the hot wind outside starting to blow up the afternoon storm. Through the window, I see papers spiral into the sky. "My work is in this too, you can't just *take* it from me, Dan!"

He nods and his pinched face is bitter. "I sure as fuck can."

I feel heat return to my body. Red-hot raging heat. I raise my fists and step forward, but he swings his right fist first. There's a crunching noise and I feel myself bouncing among red stars; it takes me moments to realise it's the bed.

"You're still fat – *and* still fucking slow, *boet*!" he shouts.

The door slams and I look up at a light, which is swinging dangerously above me, almost unmoored from its anchoring plaster. I can't move for a moment on the bed and can only hope the loose light fitting doesn't crash on top of me as well. At least that shit in reception won't have seen anything.

Dan had last hit me in high school, arguing over a board game of World Invasion; I thought we'd put all that behind us. I sit up and rub my right eye; history always seems to come back in the end.

"I'm sorry, am I interrupting anything?" (Although I haven't heard that voice in days, my blood still chills.)

I stare at the doorway with my startled left eye, right eye burning closed - outside, I hear a clap of thunder.

What an absurd announcement for the grinning face of Brand – he stands there – despite his grin, his voice is cold and clamps at me like invisible handcuffs.

"I've just met a rather upset colleague of yours," Brand says. "With something of interest to us too…"

Chapter 15
Sibusiso's Scooter

I leave the doctor on my loaned scooter, feeling sad it should be on such a sour note. Why can't we just hold onto the good that has been between us?

I drive carefully, watching the changing robots and traffic, careful not to attract attention. I have the satnav programmed for a return to Mamma, pressing the 'home' option.

Home.

Not an easy word to pin down. As the robot changes to green, I pull away, grateful for Nombuso's rushed lessons. Now I have some wheels of my own, some independence, slow though the wheels may be. Mamma has many contacts throughout the community, a little like the mother that I find hard to remember, both generous in shape and spirit.

There is a warning growl deep inside me. An old white woman crosses the road without looking, so I slow, wobbling to avoid her. Behind me, a car hoots and a man shouts in anger. He pulls up alongside me and I feel terror punch up through my bowels. It is two policemen, in a mellow-yellow van. They swerve across my path, blocking me off.

The old woman is blocked off too and looks terrified for a moment, before turning to head back the way she came. The passenger policeman steps out, thickset and business like, holding out a hairy hand, "*Dompas.*"

I give him my pass. He looks it over and gives it a slight nod, handing it back.

I almost cry with relief, but he does not move. He holds his hand out again. "Learner's License."

I scrabble in my pocket for the fake license Mamma had given me, sweating. The policeman looks at it for a moment and then fishes a cell-phone out of his pocket. He scans the license with his phone and suddenly goes very still.

He drops my license onto the floor and waves at his fellow-cop with his left hand. "Step against the vehicle, boy, spread your hands and legs."

He asks with clipped and apparent politeness, but I know there is no way I can say no.

I am eighteen. I am no boy.

Still, I spread my hands against their hot van and straddle my legs wide. I hear the jingle of handcuffs. It seems he does not even want to touch me, so he does not search me.

The other cop is opening the back of the van.

Mamma! There is no answer to the plea in my head; my arms are twisted behind me and cuffed in a painful pinch.

Inside me, a caged Beast growls, but the cops appear to hear nothing.

They book me for possession of a false license. I am relieved at first, but they will not let me go. "Wait for final clearance to leave, boy," says the police clerk, even though he is black too and only looks a little older than me.

I go back to sit on a chair in the crowded black section of the charge room; people mill in and out and I eye the door and freedom outside, but a soldier stands there, an R4 rifle slung over his shoulder. Mamma has taught me a few things about guns – mostly to stay as far away from them as possible.

I stand and saunter casually towards the door, pretending I have come in with a family, who are now leaving. I trail behind them, so they do not notice me. I catch the flash of a raised hand from behind the charge desk and the soldier steps forward, stopping me with a firm press of his hand on my right shoulder. "You stay, brother."

How can we have black policemen, black army, to enforce unjust laws against ourselves? Desperate times indeed, when brother takes up against brother, for a crust of bread.

I turn back and feel my gut tighten. A black policeman has

opened a waist high door from behind the charge desk and walks towards me with a grim face. He has a small sheet in his hand, "Sibusiso Mchunu, you are hereby under arrest for charges of terrorism and murder."

Another policeman has followed him through – this one is white and is bigger. He carries the standard handcuffs that seem deliberately too small to fit with comfort on *any* wrist.

"I have killed no one," I say, terrified yet somehow strangely pleased that my voice does not squeak. A part of me seems to hover outside my body, keeping calm despite my bowels turning with fear.

My hands are cuffed in front of me and the big white policeman pulls me by the small chain between them, chafing my wrists further. "We shall see," he says, as a large metal door opens in front of him.

"Room 619!" shouts the first cop after us.

This white cop has a bit of a paunch, so we take the lift. The lift has two cops and two other black men in tow, both looking miserable. I wonder if I look as miserable to them. (I am starting to feel so.) On the 6th floor, the white cop drags me along a corridor that is painted a cheerful pink. I want to vomit on the floor in order to paint it the colour it deserves, but I have no opportunity to do so, as the cop pulls me so hard and so insistently.

He clatters for a key with his left hand in his pocket, finally barging the heavy door open with his left shoulder.

I vomit on *this* floor though – it's red plastic, as if to hide blood. My vomit is a sticky orange-brown and the cop yanks me off my feet so that I clatter to my knees, banging them hard so that I yelp. He pulls me forward and I smell the stink of the vomit. It makes me retch again, but only a thin line of spittle comes out. "Eat it, *kaffir*," he says, but he does not push my face into my *kotch*.

It is the room that has made me sick. It is barred and bare, apart from two chairs, a hanging light and an open, stained box that looks like a set of dental tools I'd seen once, in a mobile township dental clinic. "Agggh...." the cop shouts, suddenly looking bored, yanking me to my feet and thrusting me at the one chair which has straps on it.

He pushes me back and kicks my feet from under me, so that I lose my footing and fall into the chair. He clicks the cuffs open with a key and then straps my arms onto the chair. "My teeth are fine," I say.

He looks at me blankly for a moment and then suddenly he roars with laughter, his head rocking back so that I can see his red tongue and heavy set of fillings. His right front tooth is chipped slightly in the middle too. He snaps his mouth shut and grins at me: "You're a *fokking* funny kaffir," he says. "I hope they don't kill you too quickly."

He shrugs, pockets his keys and walks out. I hear the metallic clunk of the door being locked behind him.

Only then do I cry, although I know it will do me no good.

Chapter 16
Martin's Interrogation

The charge office is quiet; a few families reporting muggings, I think, but Brand does not give me time to settle. He clicks open a solid metal door behind the office with a remote in his hand and leads me along a dark corridor, suddenly ducking into a side room. It's basic, a soft chair and a wooden bench opposite, set across a wide wooden desk – the bench has no back support. I do not need to ask where I should sit.

"Rrright!" Brand rolls his r's enthusiastically, as if keen to show he's *tweetalig*. He rubs his hands expectantly and leans back in his comfortable chair, which rocks back with his movement, with solid-looking ergonomics.

I sit and shift my buttocks. The bench is built on the thin side too, enough to cause discomfort to anyone sitting with a normal bum. I'm disadvantaged further by my fat *arse*, which is unable to find sufficient supportive purchase on the bench. Added to that, my right eye feels like it is swelling, it's stinging and closing, the vision blurring. I am not used to sitting on this side of the desk either. Although I am frightened, I need to hide this – and shift the power dynamic between us.

Somehow.

"Tell me first, Doctor, how you lost and got your Mind Box back. I have information from your colleague, but only up until the box was – lost – or perhaps given away? To *undesirables*, I believe." Brand leans forward, his hands open, clasping for information, his face benign.

Do I look like that at all, to my patients?

I stand. Keep moving, as I told Sibusiso; don't let the mongoose freeze you with its gaze.

Brand looks up, surprised, "I don't recall giving you permission to stand, Doctor."

I stretch and start trying to touch my toes. I can only get as far as my left knee. Shit, I'm going to have to get fitter; leaner is meaner. Or Brand is. He's up and around the desk in one fluid movement; his face is no longer benign, pushing up against mine.

By now I can only see through my left eye.

"Are you taking the *pisssss*, Doctor, as the English saying goes?"

"I know my rights," I say. "I get one phone call."

"Hah!" He laughs and turns to the desk, picking up a cordless receiver. "You'd better make it count, Doctor, you're in some really deep *kak*, I can tell you."

He hands me the phone, smirking. I take a card out of my back pocket and dial. Oh, I do intend to make this count.

"Helen?" I say, "It's me, Martin van Deventer. I'm being interrogated by a Mr. Brand from the Special Branch."

"A *woman*?" Brand laughs disbelievingly and sits down behind his desk, grinning.

"You haven't said anything to him yet, have you, Martin?" Her voice is as sharp as I'd remembered it.

"No," I say.

"Good. Lucky for you I've done a lot of *pro bono* representation around security legislation – and *not* on behalf of the state either."

I wait. Brand opens a file, picks up a pen and smiles back at me, tapping the empty page expectantly with his pen.

"Let me have a word with him."

I hand the phone to Brand, who takes it with his left hand and places it to his ear. "Hello, madam," he says.

I watch as his smile fades. Then he drops the pen with his free right hand. Finally, he starts to scowl. "She wants to speak to you again!" he snarls, thrusting the phone at me.

I turn my back on him. "Hello again, Helen?"

"I've sorted him out, Martin... and by the way, did you know Dan was screwing other women?"

I'm quiet, unsure what to say.

"You men, you're always fucking sticking together. Funny thing is he seemed to think you'd ratted on him, when I could smell the cheap whores on his skin... Never mind, he's had to find new accommodation for himself."

"You've split?"

"Careful, that SB bastard is probably listening. You're not out of the woods yourself yet, either. Take care, Martin. Give me a call when you're out, so we can set up a legal meeting."

I hand the phone back to Brand. He slams it down. "You're free to go. For now."

He no longer calls me Doctor, but I don't mind.

Chapter 17
Sibusiso's Interrogation

The man scares me.

He's not very big, he's thin, with straggly blond hair and moustache, but his blue eyes have no temperature. He sits opposite me, scrolling through his phone, reading text.

"Rrrright!" he says, as if preparing to use English. He puts his phone down on his chair's wide armrest and looks at me. There is only space between us – and frighteningly little of it. He leans forward and pushes the trolley of dental-looking equipment away from us.

I breathe a bit easier, repressing a sigh of relief.

He smiles.

It's a game.

With only one winner.

I close my eyes. Anything to keep his blue eyes from infiltrating me.

"You know Dr. Van Deventer, I believe?" His voice is rough, but not unkind.

I open one eye. He is scrolling through his phone again. I open the other eye.

"Yes," I say, "I was his patient at Fort Napier."

"I believe he treated you with somewhat *unorthodox* methods." He looks up at me, but I keep my eyes open. "Unorthodox means unusual."

"I know!" I feel the Beast stirring within me.

He glances up at me and smiles, "You're feisty for a boy."

I must have looked blank, because he went on: "Feisty means..."

But I don't wait for him. I rattle off a torrent of abuse in isiZulu. He looks at me blankly.

I stop. He smiles, but this time a little less smugly. "Shall I

187

call in an interpreter then?"

It's hard to shrug with these straps so tight around my arms and wrists; already I feel numb, sensation draining from my body.

He shakes his head. "I agree. Why call in an interpreter when your English is good enough to give me the information I need. One less Bantu person to witness our *special* relationship developing..."

I was wrong. His voice *is* unkind. "So," he says, "how did the good doctor treat you with his new – invention – I believe?"

"It reads minds," I say, "Lets people get below the skin. Makes them see how similar we all are."

"Hmm," He raises his right eyebrow, "My, you are a clever boy indeed. So what did you do with this doctor's box? It is, I believe like a box, no?"

I nod.

He puts down his phone and leans forward. Despite myself, I close my eyes again.

"So. Where did you go, with this box? And did the doctor give it to you?"

I open my left eye in surprise. "No, he didn't – I, uh, *took* it."

He smiles, but only slightly: "So *where* did you take it, Sibusiso?"

His use of my name throws me slightly and I have to stop myself answering. It seems rehearsed too, and slides off his tongue as if he's familiar with *isiZulu*. But he did not blink when I'd called his mother a bitch with three balls. It's hard to believe he could be *so* controlled.

"*Where*, Sibusiso?" He leans forward and I smell meat on his breath; biltong, I think. I almost want to laugh at the stereotype, but I know laughing will only make things worse.

"I can't remember," I say.

"Ohhh," and he leans back, "of course not."

The stench of his breath lingers and I want to be sick again, but I feel hollow, empty, without feeling. The numbness is seeping down my spine now. It feels as if my body is floating above me, looking down on some poor sucker strapped by his arms to a chair, with no hope of escape.

The man turns and pulls the trolley of dental-looking tools closer to us. He picks up a narrow sharp looking pincer tool and inspects it closely.

He holds it up to me, wagging it, as if he is thinking, and then speaks, "Did you know I failed dental school before I joined the police, boy? I don't know why. Shall we find out?"

"No," I say.

"Good," he says. "So where did you go?"

I am floating no longer. Instead, I'm trapped in a terrified body, a Beast prowling inside me, but helplessly - watching a Beast smile in front of me, taunting me with a scary piece of metal.

His phone rings.

I sob.

He picks up the receiver, speaking in rapid Afrikaans I can follow. "*Ja?* I told you not to disturb me. Alright then, you've finally confiscated it? Good. Bring it here."

He switches the phone off and gives me a long, discomfiting look, "I'm a civilized man, Sibusiso" he says, "We'll do things the gentle way, shall we?"

I nod, unsure of what he means.

The door opens. A policeman stands there, holding the doctor's Mind Box.

The blond man puts his phone and sharp tool down, stands up and rubs his hands. "Ex-cell-ent! Let's see how well this works, shall we?"

I hear the Beast inside me roar.

But the man opposite me hears nothing, as he fixes the wired caps to our scalps. It looks as if he's done his homework on how this works.

He smiles as he flicks the dial on the doctor's Box.

Chapter 18
Martin's Visit

I return Gertie's car with thanks, a bottle of Cape red, and a pipe with psychedelic swirls on it. From the James' house, I phone work and apologise to the Principal Psychologist for three days unannounced and unauthorized absence. I'd seen him at the OASS meeting – and thankfully he's very forgiving, as if he has some inside information on my difficulties.

I call Jabula ward then – Jabu is finishing up his shift and I arrange to collect Jacky. First, though, Gertie kindly drops me at the hospital, where I collect my car, embrace Jabu, and follow his car to his small terraced township home. Jacky gives me a huge greeting, leaping up and scrabbling at me, even though she has obviously been well cared for. I stay for a meal with Jabu's generous family and we joke about my black eye.

I get home, home sweet home, completely exhausted at 8.08 p.m.

Jacky's on my lap as I sit on the couch, brain dead, watching TV, which is hinting at secret peace talks with the ANC.

"Shit." I tell her cocked retriever-cross face, her brown eyes fixed on mine, as if wondering why I haven't brought my usual sweet snack to watch the news with, "Things are starting to move bloody quickly."

My cell rings and I fumble it out of my pocket. The number is withheld. "Martin?"

"Yes?" the voice is feminine and familiar.

"It's Sally Jones here. We have heard that the police have Sibusiso. Special Agent Brand is leading the interrogation."

Shit, shit, shit. I briefly wonder how she has my number, but that's irrelevant now.

"I can't visit him; they want me very badly. I hear you've got some legal clearance. Can you please help him and… and, send him my love?"

She sounds choked, vulnerable, unlike the powerful, collected woman I had spoken to somewhere in the heart of *Imbali* a few nights ago.

"Sure," I say, "Which police station?"

"'Maritzburg Central. And... Doctor?"

"Yes..." I say warily, waiting for a punch-line, alerted by her use of my title.

"They have him on a serious charge. They may well kill him, trying to extract information."

I can't speak.

"Doctor –?" her voice has regained its sharpness and assertion, "We have thirty seconds before they can trace this. I'm sure they have a lock on your phone."

I finger the memory stick in my pocket and an idea shoots up my fingers and into my brain; but it's a long shot indeed. "Uh, Sally, do you have anyone who's good with the internet? I'm talking really good."

There's the shortest of pauses. "I can think of just the man," she says.

"I've got something I need to get onto the external World Wide Web, through the State firewalls. It's valuable – and dense, very dense, a heavy file indeed."

"Say no more," Mamma says. She hangs up, but not before I feel the buzz of a cell-phone in my pocket.

The 'emergency' phone she gave me when we last met.

I pull it out, memorise the address displayed on the screen and then delete the text.

This trip, I make on my own.

I am frightened, but know it is nothing compared to what Sibusiso faces.

Address keyed into my satnav, I drive towards *Imbali* Township. The roads darken as electrification from the white suburbs recedes behind me.

I swerve to avoid a stray dog scuttling across the road. To the side of the road, hovering at the edge of my widest headlight beam, shacks and then small but more solid brick houses flash past in the gloom around me. There are only a few men walking the dusty track on the sides of the streets, as if everyone fears the dark.

Not though, it seems, the car behind me. It has followed me at a discreet distance for a while now, but given there is little traffic in the township I cannot miss its dipped beams.

I pull over and wait.

So does the car behind me, switching its lights off.

Darkness drops a black cloak over it.

I see nothing and no one.

I hit the accelerator in terror and swerve back onto the road, swinging down a narrow alley that almost seems too small for a car. I see headlights flash onto the road behind me, but I have swung randomly right, then left, then right again; the lights have disappeared.

The roads have opened into what appears to be a small market area, and I pull my car behind a large container, with a cell logo – *VodaGaan* – daubed on its side.

I switch off my lights and engine and wait.

Silence.

No one walks these streets at night it seems.

Sweat sticks my shirt to the back of my seat – I sit forward and peel myself off with a slow and sticky wrench.

I jump as the Satnav clicks at me in what sounds like Xhosa, the language facility evidently bounced off Afrikaans by the swerves and bumps in the road.

The satnav has rerouted itself and I see I am not too far off from a chequered flag on the screen.

Thank the Gods for GPS!

Still silence.

There is no sign of any car lights, so I pull off slowly and turn down a side street, switching off the satnav so that the car rolls to a halt near a small house, one window glowing with light.

I see a large woman standing at the foot of a few stairs leading up into the house.

I switch off my lights and shiver. My car is locked, my windows rolled up. I can't quite believe I have not been jumped from the darkness by white men with *sjamboks* and pistols – or black men with AK-47 rifles.

I start as Sally Jones knocks on my window. She has a torch in her left hand.

"Come on, Martin, get out of there, we have too little time."

I step out of the car and she bounds up the few stairs, waving me on with an impatient shimmy of light from her left hand.

I remember the small entrance hall and seating space, lit by gas-lamps, but she guides me into the room on the left without hesitation.

It's a deceptively big room, with a large bed to one side, a small child-like figure sleeping on the bed. Across from the bed though are a set of jury-rigged computers, chaotically connected with plugs sprouting through the floor.

A man is sitting there, but gets up as I walk in. He is short but stocky and powerful, dressed in anonymous trousers and unmarked T-shirt of uncertain colour in the flickering light.

"Xolile, this is Martin – Martin, Xolile." She steps aside so that we can shake. I am not sure I can pronounce his name properly, so say nothing.

The man drops his hand with distaste: "Now that is what I call a wet handshake."

"I think I was followed, but lost them," I croaked.

Sally barks a command behind me and a woman with a rifle, perhaps Nombuso, rushes past the door.

I turn to Xolile.

"What have you got for me?" His voice is a growl, but sounds surprisingly relaxed and friendly.

I hand him the stick and he plugs it into a port.

I whistle and wave at the set up.

"Informally sponsored by the white Council's power grid," he grins at me, "…and was that a job to get done."

He turns to the screen and his mouth opens at the file that pops onto the screen.

"What sort of shit is this?"

"It's Sibusiso," I say, "Or a few of his thoughts at least. Reckon you can get him onto the outside web?"

He frowns. "Maybe, maybe, maybe… One hell of a job though, it'll take time. There's going to be lots of bridges to build."

He locks his fingers together and splays them against each other, cracking his knuckles.

"You got a close of day score at Newlands, Martin?"

I am incredulous, "You follow white provincial cricket?"

"No, Doctor." He turns to the screen and sits down. "I just follow cricket."

Sally laughs softly behind my left shoulder.

My heart sinks with a stark thought, "No one will be able to read the file."

Xolile doesn't even look up from his screen, "That's why I'm sending the free Chinese neural app with it."

Sally throttles another laugh beside me.

As I've said before, I've given up believing I know everything – or even anything at all.

I watch Xolilie's fingers fly over the keyboard, but am really listening to the sound of a few crickets outside and the distant yammering of dogs.

And I think of Sibusiso as his brain waves are sent across the world, a man who I had once thought of as 'just a young Bantu man' – and I am ashamed, very ashamed.

They allow me ten minutes with him.

Ten freaking minutes.

I'd called Helen, who'd rung them up, but even their lawyer had bounced her. They were apparently gathering double murder evidence. Two policemen apparently, so no legal wiggle room on that at all.

But *not* Sibusiso?

He sits the other side of a small glass peephole; a metal barrier between us. We talk as if we both know we're being recorded, so there's no way I'm relaying anything from 'Sally Jones'. I have no intention of digging myself in any deeper.

His face is tired, drawn and he looks as if he's in pain. "You look like shit, Doctor," he says, though. "Were you beaten up by a new girlfriend?"

I smile, although both eyes sting. Keep a lid on it, van Deventer.

"What have they done to *you*, Sibusiso?"

"Taking information." He winces. It looks as if each word costs him energy too.

Perhaps even ten minutes is more than he can manage in his current condition. Bastards – fucking, fucking bastards!

"It's absurd; they say you've been involved in a double murder."

"Not true," he says, but I spot the brief eye flicker. Fuckit, he's in *much* deeper than me.

I know better than to touch that topic again. "You're still under the hospital," I say. "Professor Pillay, our Principal Psychologist, is filing for an emergency psychiatric transfer."

"Thanks," he says; but every word seems to diminish him just a little more, his face sinks slightly lower.

"Is there anything I can do for you in the meantime, Sibusiso? *Anything?*"

He looks at me; his eyes are puffy, his face swollen. And then he starts to cry; just very big, very slow drops. "Just my father," he says. "Please just call my father."

I cannot touch him. The glass is a dumb impenetrable barrier between us.

"Sure... sure, Sibusiso."

"And Doctor?"

"Martin," I say.

"And Martin, they were – uh, very cross to find your machine is not perfect. I found a way to... to manage it."

Dan had no doubt handed our Box over without a word.

But Sibusiso carries on speaking, squeezing his words out. "You just think of one thing very hard, Doctor, just hold one vital thought that keeps everything else away. My father..." He does not finish his sentence; he has sunk too low, he's sobbing too hard.

He flashes a wave at me through the glass – and is then gone.

It is several minutes before I can move. I don't give a fuck about any hidden cameras.

I know for certain I will not be able to visit Sibusiso again.

Not unless I had the smallest of hopes to offer – perhaps a legal reprieve, perhaps the gathering of outside aid, if Xolile is able to get Sibusiso's thoughts out onto the free world wide web.

For now though, I have nothing.

I snarl at the warden who asks me to leave.

Chapter 19
Room 619 and Sibusiso's Cell

Room 619 again.

I have heard more of it since I first came here.

This is a hard room indeed, a room high in the skies where nothing or no one can be heard.

And no one leaves room 619 – everyone knows that.

At least, not without spilling all of their secrets – along with their soul…

…And just a little bit of blood, gristle, and (I've heard) bone.

The metal door clangs behind me and my heart sinks at the rusty red vinyl floor, designed not to need a frequent wash. I smell the stale stink of shit, my good left eye flickering across the flat looking room in vain search of anchors of hope, before my own bowels dissolve. The walls stay a stained yellow, marred with a few darker scrabbling fingerprints.

There is just a small wooden desk in the middle, a lone light bulb hanging overhead and two chairs on either side. One is a comfy looking leather chair, but I am not fooled, I see the straps hanging from its armrests. The second chair is small and has its wooden back to me; it is filled with a small, lithe looking white man. I just see the back of his crew-cut blond hair, as he bends over the desk, typing into his flickering O-Pad. He wears a grey suit.

Me, I wear nothing but handcuffs.

Shall I rush him and club him with my cuffs? Does he even know I am here?

The wooden chair swivels and the man smiles up at me. I recognise Brand again, chief of the local Special Branch.

My bowels threaten to evacuate, but I hold them firm with a fierce clench of my teeth and anus. I will show this man nothing, not even my waste.

197

"Ahhh, Sibusiso," he stands and smiles, "Sorry to see my colleagues have been a bit – uh – firm in their handling of you. Never fear, I will look after you *much* better."

I turn my head to allow my left eye to scan the shadows. We are alone together in this small cell, the security policeman and I.

Is he a fool?

I lift my arms, but with one quick motion he has levered me across the floor and swung me into the chair. Dimly, I feel him strapping my arms down, remembering the injection they gave me this morning and how hard it has been to move and think thereafter.

The man stands and smiles again and I feel all hope evaporate into the shitty air around me.

He tells me that Mandela has died an old and broken man on *Robben Island* and no one else cares about our struggle. It is time for me to tell him who my accomplices are, what we know about the police and the army – who are now camped in our townships. What are the names of our informers, what it is we plan to do... And what sorts of things do my sisters like?

He smiles again when I stir at the last one. He's not a nice man; a blond man, an ice man, suited in steel grey. His blue eyes are dead to me.

But for sure he is no fool.

Still, I can see he is tiring from my lack of response, "You see this Box again?"

It is the doctor's Mind Box. The Box is a foot square and squats between us like an ugly toad. I see two switches, a dial and a gauge on its one side. On both sides of the Box lie a set of coiled leads attached to a thin hair-net.

He must remember I can block my mind.

He picks up one of the nets and rubs it softly, "Electrodes my boy, all primed to relay your thoughts directly into my head – all of your deepest darkest secrets."

"Why can't secrets be light?"

"Eh –?" He looks at me with a moment of bafflement and

then barks a short laugh, just like a brown hyena. "Funny man. Shall we see if I can suck your soul, boy?"

I am no boy. I am eighteen.

Does he joke with me? It is clear he cannot yet hear my thoughts. I must be careful now, all fuzzy headed as I am.

Brand steps forward and wraps the net over my head, fastening it tight and painfully with sticky suckers underneath my ears.

He steps back with distaste and wipes his hands with a white handkerchief from his left breast pocket. Theatrically he drops the cloth and grinds it underneath his heel. He then picks up the other lead and clips the set of electrodes onto his short *boere*-cut blond head. Brand flicks the switch on the Black Box from a standing position, leads pulled away from the table and coiling into the laced cap on his head. He stands as far away as he can, as if I smell of *kak*, of dog shit even – but perhaps he just thinks that of all black men.

As for me, I have no choice. The chair is bolted to the floor, my forearms strapped to the armrests.

"Again, who are your comrades?" He barks at me, trying to lance me with his eyes, but I close my good eye and join the blood-stained darkness.

He laughs then; "This time will be different boy. We've drugged you, to the point of unconsciousness, where there is no defence... There can be no resistance when you are almost *fokking* asleep."

My thoughts are swirling up like papers on a black breeze, I cannot control the wind.

All I can do is shape what is found on those papers. I focus on one paper, zooming in, enlarging the picture. The pixelated picture steadily sharpens within me – and I am lost in reality.

I sit... beside Father (?) as we fish a stream near the *Ukhahlamba* Mountains. He bends his carved rod playfully, laughing that he has caught a shark. For brief seconds I scrabble at the grassy bank beneath us, trying to get away, but I stop at his guffaws of laughter.

He grabs my leg and pulls me back down again. I see by his face it is yet another of his jokes.

I smile and relax, picking up my rod again.

"See, my boy!" Father points up, as a large brown bird circles above us, swooping in to land on the other bank. It is an ugly bird, with a wedge shaped head and strutting manner.

"*Uthekwana*," he says, "Lightning Bird – the *boere* call it the Hamerkop. A bad bird, perhaps sent by a witch – and a powerful one indeed, as it can burn a place down with its lightning bolts."

The bird looks vaguely familiar but I still laugh, for I am well educated and have lost belief in such magical things.

The bird stands on the far bank and watches us with keen interest. There is something strangely familiar – yet distant – about those eyes, as the bird tilts its big bill to peer across at us. Father has stood and throws a rock across to the other side. The bird shrieks, leaps and takes flight.

I stand up to hold back his arm, my heart strangely tugged skywards by that peculiar bird.

Father only asks, looking ahead: "So, who are your comrades, my boy?"

I turn to look at him and catch his sidewards glance. Surely Father does not have *blue* eyes?

I pick up the rod and cast. "Shall we catch a whale instead of a shark?" I ask him.

The breeze picks up around us and I avoid looking at the urgent scraps of debris flying past us, afraid of what they might reveal.

All I see is the green rippled surface of the stream and smell the sweet smell of a *dagga* pipe he has lit up, as he stands beside me.

"I am proud of you, my boy." He pats my arm. "Who are your best friends at college?"

I turn and look down at him, realising with sudden vertigo how much he has shrunk. Still, his eyes are now reassuringly brown. Perhaps I did not see correctly? What is bothering me?

He drags on his pipe and offers me the stem.

I shake my head and the sweet giddying smoke coils between us.

The wind is rising and my rod has caught nothing.

Father looks so small and shrunken and I have a sense I have not seen him for a long time – and a fear I will never see him again.

I drop the rod and hug him.

He pats my back: "I am indeed proud of you – I am guessing you have good friends to tell me about, my son."

I open my mouth as we release each other... and stop. He is looking at me, perhaps just a little *too* closely?

"First... Tell me about my mother, Father."

He pushes me away with surprising strength for such a small, frail looking man. "What? Why?"

I look down at him. His creased face is crumpled with surprise. "I miss her so badly, Father, even though I have only shadowy memories of her. Please tell me more about her, what was she like? How did you meet?"

He opens his mouth, but nothing comes out.

I am so sad.

It is as if he won't... or perhaps *can't* tell me.

All I remember is mother holding me close and calling me 'Biso, telling me how much she loved me, after she became ill.

That's when her swearing got worse too – Father always remonstrated with her about this, even when she was too sick to eat... But *this* father can tell me nothing.

The sadness starts to fill my chest. The wind bursts past us and through us in a surging howl of distress. We stagger for moments and his body is torn from me, lifted up over the bank, careening into a low hanging fever tree.

As for me, I lie flat on the bank, elbows braced against the rough grassed crest, screaming after him. His body lies still, his eyes closed. Yet all I can do is think of my mother.

I cry as rain pours down on me.

Something is stripped off my head and I gasp at the burning light above my blinking eye.

"*Wat die fok* are you doing, boy?"

It is Brand who stands over me, his lips twisted with rage, but his eyes are leaking. Or... crying too?

He flings his right arm across his face and swings abruptly round to leave the room, forgetting to untie me.

The metal door clangs shut and I am left with myself and the stale smelly air.

What...?

It hits me then.

Brand must have lost someone too.

I listen to the distant high chatter of a ghostly *uthekwana* bird, flitting beyond the walls, but growing softer and more distant all the time.

Mama?

It has been quiet for a very long time, I think, before the warden comes in to release me and take me back to my cell.

This time stepping stiffly in to Room 619, I close the door quietly behind me, spirits lifted a bit that I am unshackled and have been allowed to wear some blue corduroy shorts.

The vision in my painful right eye is blurred but sufficiently good enough to allow me some depth perception and I am surprised as to how *big* the room actually is. Much bigger than the cell I have lived in for almost six months now, with no trial as yet in sight.

The man sitting in the small wooden chair with his back to me is not Brand.

He pushes the stool back, stands up and turns to me.

He is a dark man, perhaps even darker than me. And I can see he is also not a nice man – a dead man, suited in neatly efficient blue overalls, but with a smart grey jacket on top. His brown eyes do not even bother to look at me.

"Detective Brand is busy elsewhere and has asked me to take over our conversation," he tells me in isiZulu., "He also tells me you're a smart shit and that I must be careful. These white men can be funny can't they, *umfaan*?"

I do not smile. I am not his friend.

I can tell by the way he holds himself I have no chance against him physically. Where would I run to anyway? Room 619 is always bolted behind me, with an armed guard outside. Hope has long since emptied itself from my chest.

The large man gestures me into the leather seat and I hold back a wince as he hangs heavily on the straps before securing them.

"What is your name, brother?" I ask, hoping for a label to hang onto.

All he does is sit and stare at me.

"I have no name," he says eventually – and I know this will be a long afternoon.

Between us, the Black Box sits, a dark hole in a dark room, the bulb above us is dull and flickering erratically as if it is about to die. I find myself trying to find a pattern in the flickering light and silence, but there is none.

The man with no name continues to stare as if waiting for me to talk, so I oblige him.

"Why do you fight for the white man when all he does is abuse us? Why do you not fight for us, your own people, my brother?" My words are muffled by the swelling of my lips, but I can see he has caught my meaning.

He leans back in his chair and pats his belly, bulging against his overalls. "You are sharp on only one side, like a knife. I have no wish to be one of the wretched of the Earth, my *brother*."

I do not think of myself as so clever, but I guess that he has also been in our training camps – perhaps in Angola, perhaps in Zambia.

"*Askari!*" I snap and he smiles for the first time, albeit a brief rictus of his lips.

"Let's get on with this, shall we?" He looks bored, standing up to reach across and clip the electrodes onto my head. "Let's explore this unknown land inside your head, no?"

He fastens his own net-scalp and then sits down heavily, flicking the switch with the thick thumb on his left hand. He, at least, sits opposite me, now inviting a level gaze.

I dig my fingers into my palms, resisting the surge of drugged sleep.

Then I give it to him, holding my mind still, empty, calm. I stare at the shiny surface of his brown eyes; his left eye slightly darker than the right one, the whites of his eyes a faded yellow. I stare and share our struggles, our pain, our fight, but keeping it distant, remote, away from any names that may be caught and harmed.

And he laughs.

He laughs so much he is doubled over in his chair, capped head resting on the table between us.

I realise that not even the flies are his friends.

The table quivers with his laughter and I jerk my head back sharply. Pain shreds my scalp as the leads snap tight against the Black Box, which slides and judders on the shaking table. I watch without breathing as it teeters, about to fall, to break, and to end any further sharing of anything at all.

The man's big right hand snatches across to hold the Box firm and his left hand steadies the table. He is half-standing, leaning forward with his menacing weight, and he is no longer laughing.

He looks straight at me and I feel terror. The lead hangs like an electrical whip around his shoulders; in his steady eyes, I see my end. He rips the lead from my head and holds it like a garrotte between his hands.

This, I cannot win.

I close my eyes.

He laughs again, a low rolling chuckle.

Terrified, I shout Mother's name.

But she is long dead and I am indeed just a silly boy.

In the darkness, I sense the man hesitating.

My eyes are wet when I open them.

The *Askari* has stripped the leads from his scalp and is standing straight, but looking at the door.

A shadow without solid form stands there, a deeper darkness that swirls and – as it gathers density – slowly takes shape.

The *Askari* fists the leads in his right hand, rubbing his eyes with his left, but then swings to face me.

"What *muti* have you slipped me, boy? What poison has your mind fed me?"

But it is the bird I watch – a big bird – strutting towards us both, with long, thick bill and serious intent.

The man swears and swings a boot at her, but there is only empty air.

We are alone in the gloom.

He gives a shuddering laugh and then turns to me.

"I don't know what the fuck that was – but I will give you one last fucking chance. Think about it, all alone in your fucking cell. Tomorrow, if you do not speak, you do not live. Stay fucking well, friend…"

He knocks and the door opens. He straightens his jacket sleeves as he leaves.

As for me, I am shaking.

I just know for sure the… bird… was female.

I know too from the Psych One course at college that we both saw it – 'consensual validation' they call it – reality.

Can it really be?

"Mama!" I weep, but the only answer I get is the warden coming in to release me, for what I know will be the last time.

He gives me a tissue, even though he is busy flicking through his cell menu with his right thumb and I catch the flash of internet porn.

As for me, I don't wipe my face, fearful I might wipe *her*

away as well.
> Mother.
> Busisiwe.

This is not a bad cell, even though I am alone here.

It has a reed mat, although a little short for me. But it has a soft mattress, which eases the burns and bruises on my back just a bit. Such little bits are always very welcome.

And it has a rough grey blanket, which I fold neatly every morning.

The cell even has a tiny wooden bookshelf, a little crooked, although I have no books.

The reed mat is a little thin maybe, but it takes some of the sting out of the soles of my feet too.

Most of all, though, it has a window – broken by my fist – but there is no way out through those bars, so they have spent no rands on replacing it.

And the little window looks down on a courtyard. A concrete courtyard where we walk three times a day, stretching our limbs, smelling the breeze and slapping our bare feet – often wet on the last of the day's walk, in the aftermath of the evening summer storms.

And in the middle of the courtyard is a tree. A big tree, but struggling and bent, surrounded by wire fencing, so that prisoners can't touch it.

Through the window, through the bars, I watch birds dance in the scraggly branches as the sun sinks low.

Then they are gone.

I look around – oh yes, and there is a toilet too, a hole in the floor on the side of the cell, with an ineffectual cord to flush the worst of my blood and shit away.

The sun has disappeared, as it does. A few clouds cluster in the growing damp darkness.

I only half-hear the rattle of slop on a tin plate being pushed through the flap in my door – for lately I am becoming fearful of *ukudlisa*, both bewitchment and poisoning, even though my mind is modern.

So indeed it has been a good while since I have either eaten or been hungry.

A half-moon starts to leak through the bars.

I record the last of my thoughts and place the digi-disc from Father on the bookshelf, wiped clean of the inside of my bowels.

Room 619 tugs my thoughts and I know the end for me is very near.

No one leaves room 619.

Everyone knows that.

I sink to my knees.

There it is again – a high pitched, but brief, squawking sound – and this time it comes from outside my window.

I crawl and drag myself up against the window bars.

For desperate moments, I see nothing and am frightened I am losing sight in both eyes now. Then milky moonlight bleeds softly into my eyes and I see the tree.

I am not alone.

Perched ungainly on the top, swaying slightly in the breeze, is the squat shape of the *uthekwana* bird. She turns her shovel shaped head and stares at me with black-holed eyes, just for the briefest moment – and then she leaps and flaps into the darkness above.

The swirl of her wings whips a breeze through my broken window.

She calls me from the night sky and I know she is heading for a river or lake, high up, over on the *Ukhahlamba* Mountains.

There is no way to follow and I turn back to my small but familiar cell.

It is indeed not a bad room.

I know every burning, aching bump of that floor mattress. In the end, I have always found a way to fall asleep.

But, after this night, there will be no more sleep – unless I talk.

The faint cries of the *uthekwana* bird are fading on the wind.

I cannot talk.

But I want to live.

And I am so tired of being alone.

My body feels like a shadow as I turn back to the window.

There is a way out – but it is too small.

Am I mad? Or am I dying? I have a sense I must do the impossible, if I can only just believe enough.

I take a deep breath and close my eyes, crunching my shoulders together, butting the bars with my face. I squeeze, harder and harder, until the pain lances hotly along my cheeks and I feel blood leak onto my shoulders as my ears rip slowly off my head, with a white-hot shredding noise. My nose is long and hard though, punching out the last of the glass pane - and with a desperate shriek I pull, lever and kick myself up and through the window.

Glass shreds my arms and sides and I scream and tumble downwards.

It is six stories down.

I do not want to die, so I open my broken arms.

And, catching the last gasp of a dying thermal, I soar upwards.

I am… *flying?*

I hear a loud shriek in the sky above me, a flash of light spurts down from the muggy darkness.

Below me, the prison ignites, with an explosive and fiery detonation. *uMgungundlovu* Prison burns, as if with the fires of Hell.

Red-orange flames sprout and roar and I smell the hot stench of rising smoke.

– and it seems even room 619 burns.

As for me, I spread my wings and spiral higher on the heat of those flames, trailing feathers and blood.

My mother calls ahead of me and I follow, as we fly on through dark and wet clouds, to new lands where I have never been.

In the muggy darkness I sense a host of us following *Mama*, ghost birds on the wing.

It is then *Unkulunkulu* speaks, a Voice from out of the darkness above: "Speak Sibusiso – name your friends and bring them back to life – give them substance alongside you in their flight – all of you, comrades on the wing."

Birds do not speak easily, so I open my mind instead to give weight to the many of my friends who have fought alongside me in the Struggle. It will be good to have their company on this journey ahead, which I sense will also be a long and hard one.

Screeching and shooting from out of the clouds in front of me comes Mother and I spin and roll to avoid her sharp beak, as she hurtles past.

"Say nothing," she says, "Trust no one."

"Even you, Mama?"

"Especially me," she swings around and flies on ahead, "I died, remember?"

I hesitate. Yes. I remember.

"Speak! Bring your friends to life now – or else you fly on alone." The Voice is from the darkness and I see no one.

How can I trust the darkness?

I sigh and bend my wings, beating hard to catch my mother, the cold murk around me now sadly empty.

So it is we sweep out of the clouds and Mother is climbing, climbing, high into the sky in the face of huge snow-capped mountains, glowing gold in a new dawn.

"I'm not an Egyptian vulture, I can't fly so high," I call after her.

Mother's voice floats back to me on the cold breeze. "I'd say you're doing fucking well just getting off the ground, 'Biso – from now on, it's just a matter of scale and effort."

"Stay, Sibusiso. I can keep you alive. But if you fly any further you will die!"

It is *Unkulunkulu* again, a Voice from the sky above me –

and I sense God speaks some truth too. No, I do not wish to die.

Mama has become a dot in the icy sky as she climbs, as if looking to find a way through the Barrier of Spears, the *Ukhahlamba* Mountains that seem intent on staring us down.

"'Biso…" filters down from above.

So high – and I just want to live.

I hesitate and hang on the air, torn between the sucking vortices of two competing voices – and one of them carries the stamp of God.

But there is so much in a name – and *how* words are spoken.

"I'm fucking coming, Mamma!"

So I strain and beat the air again, climbing higher and higher in the teeth of a wind beating off the mountain face. My wings ache, but up and up I fly, steadfastly ignoring the Call of God.

Cosi cosi iyaphela… Here, I rest my story...

Chapter 20
Message Spinning Across the Free Internet:

Sibusiso Mchunu is Alive and Well... On the Web
(Free Mchunu...!) #BlackLivesCount

About the Author

Nick Wood is a Zambian born, South African naturalised clinical psychologist, with over a dozen short stories previously published in *Interzone*, the NewCon Press anthology *Subterfuge*, *Infinity Plus*, *PostScripts* and *Redstone Science Fiction* amongst others.

Nick has also appeared in the first African anthology of science fiction, *AfroSF* – and has followed this up with a collaborative novella co-written with Tade Thompson, which appears in *AfroSF2*. *Azanian Bridges* is his debut novel.

Nick has completed an MA in Creative Writing (SF & Fantasy) through Middlesex University, London. He is currently training clinical psychologists and counsellors at the University of East London in England. Nick can be found at: @nick45wood or http://nickwood.frogwrite.co.nz/

Marcher
Chris Beckett

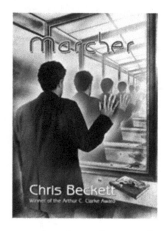

Marcher is Chris Beckett's most powerful and socially aware work to date. Drawing on his experience as a social worker and lecturer, the author paints a chilling picture of the treatment of 'others', those who don't conform, in a re-imagined Britain that is uncomfortably close to our own.

Charles Bowen is an immigration officer with a difference: the migrants he deals with don't come from other countries but from other timelines. They bring with them a mysterious drug called slip which breaks down the boundary between what is and what might be, offering the desperate and the dispossessed the hope of escape and threatening to undermine the established order.

Bowen struggles to keep track of his place in the world and to uphold the values of the system he has fought so long to maintain but is increasingly coming to question.

One of Britain's most innovative science fiction writers, Chris Beckett is the winner of the 2009 Edge Hill Prize for his short fiction and the 2013 Arthur C Clarke Award for best novel.

"Beckett explores the conservative, fear-driven mentality of restriction and repression... Beckett's hall of mirrors could not be more timely. When pressure becomes unbearable something has to give." – *Amazing Stories*

The Moon King
Neil Williamson

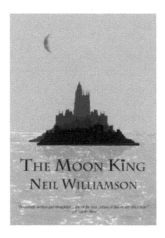

All is not well in Glassholm. Amidst rumours of unsettling dreams and strange whispering children, society threatens to disintegrate into unrest and violence. The sea has turned against them and the island's luck monkeys have gone wild, distributing new fates to all and sundry. Turmoil is coming…

"*The Moon King* is a mysterious, luminous read, full of intriguing characters... Beautifully written and thoughtful. Sure to be one of the best debuts of this or any other year." – *Jeff Vandermeer*

"*The Moon King* is adult, literary fantasy at its best."
– *The Guardian*

"The sort of book that creeps into your dreams."
– *Chris Beckett*

"*The Moon King* has you hooked from the start."
– *Edinburgh Book Review*

"*The Moon King* is wonderfully inventive and thought-provoking. Its colorful setting and rush of ideas places *The Moon King* in the top tier of fantasy debuts this year and makes Neil Williamson an author worth watching…" – *Strange Horizons*

"*The Moon King* is a deeply impressive work from a talented writer." – *SFCrowsnest*

IMMANION PRESS
Purveyors of Speculative Fiction

Legenda Maris by Tanith Lee

The sea... restless, eerie, all-powerful and mysterious – occasionally she reveals her secrets.

Legenda Maris comprises eleven tales of the ocean and her denizens, including two that are original to this collection – 'Leviathan' and 'Land's End, The Edge of The Sea' – which were among the last stories Tanith Lee wrote. In this treasure chest of tales, the author works her beguiling, linguistic sorcery to conjure mermaids who are as deadly as they are lovely, the hidden coves of lonely fishing villages harbouring mysteries, and fantastical ships that haunt the waves. She explores the relationship between the sea and the land, and the occasional meetings between those who dwell above and below the waters – meetings that are sometimes wondrous and sometimes fatal, often both.
ISBN: 978-1-907737-67-1 £11.99, $17.99

The Moonshawl by Storm Constantine

Ysbryd drwg... the bad ghost. Hired by Wyva, the phylarch of the Wyvachi tribe, Ysobi goes to Gwyllion to create a spiritual system based upon local folklore, but soon discovers some of that folklore is out of bounds, taboo... Secrets lurk in the soil of Gwyllion, and the old house Meadow Mynd. The fields are soaked in blood and echo with the cries of those who were slaughtered there, almost a century ago. Old hatreds and a thirst for vengeance have been awoken by the approaching coming of age of Wvya's son, Myvyen. If the harling is to survive, Ysobi must lay the ghosts to rest and scour the tainted soil of malice. But the ysbryd drwg is strong, built of a century of resentment and evil thoughts. Is it too powerful, even for a scholarly hienama with Ysobi's experience and skill? *The Moonshawl* is a standalone supernatural story, set in the world of Storm Constantine's ground-breaking, science fantasy Wraeththu mythos. ISBN: 978-1-907737-62-6 £11.99, $20.99

Immanion Press
http://www.immanion-press.com
info@immanion-press.com